31 DAYS OF HORROR

SHORT HORROR STORIES

ANSH ... IAL

INDIA • SINGAPORE • MALAYSIA

ISBN 979-8-89906-940-6

Dedication & Acknowledgments

For Dhir—

my brightest light in all the shadows I create.

And to the quiet horrors—

the ones that whispered first,

and taught me to listen.

To my WW—

for grounding the chaos and loving the storyteller behind the stories.

To everyone who ever turned off the lights… and then turned them back on.

To the readers who live for chills, the friends who fueled the fear, and the voices in my head that became stories on paper.

To the ones who stayed up late with me—not knowing they were helping build nightmares worth reading.

To the mirror that blinked back. The house that creaked louder when I paused.

And the whispers that said, "Write it down."

And to my son—

Dhir, may your dreams always be brighter than the darkest stories I tell.

Sections & Story Notes

Part I: Haunted & Possessed

When the dead don't rest, and the shadows remember your name...

These are stories where homes breathe, dolls whisper, and memories bite.

Part II: Curses & Rituals

Every chant, every symbol—some doors should never be opened.

These are the echoes of ancient oaths, and the screams that follow them.

Part III: Creatures & Beasts

Fangs, claws, and whispers in the dark—nature has its own nightmares.

Sometimes, it's not ghosts you need to fear... it's what's still alive.

Part IV: Distorted Realities

Sanity cracks. Time bends. Welcome to the mind's worst corners.

Where mirrors lie, roads loop, and nothing is what it seems.

Contents

Part I:
Haunted & Possessed

The Baby

October in rural Ontario, Canada, was always beautiful. The red and orange leaves fluttered through the cool air, scattering across lonely roads. But for **Emily Carter**, October would never be the same after that one fateful night.

Emily and her husband **Daniel** had been trying for a baby for years. After countless disappointments, Emily stopped hoping altogether. But one evening, **out of nowhere**, she heard a **knock on the door**.

It was October 14th, and the evening light was fading into dusk. When Emily opened the door, she found **a baby**—no more than a few months old—**wrapped in a worn, pale blanket**. There was no one in sight, only the sound of the autumn breeze whistling through the trees.

She knelt down, heart racing, and picked up the baby. **He was warm, quiet, and strangely calm**, as if he had been waiting just for her.

There was no note, no sign of who had left him, but something deep inside Emily whispered:

"This baby is meant for you."

Against all reason, she cradled him to her chest and whispered, **"It's okay, sweet boy. You're safe now."**

Emily named the baby **Oliver**. She didn't tell anyone about him—not Daniel, not the neighbors. It felt too surreal. **He was perfect**, after all. His big brown eyes followed her everywhere, and he never cried, never fussed. At night, he would lie peacefully in his crib, watching her with an unsettling stillness. But Emily didn't care.

For the first time in years, she felt **whole**.

But soon, strange things started happening around the house. Emily noticed that **the clocks always stopped at 3:15 AM**. Lights flickered, and on some nights, **the baby monitor would pick up faint whispers**, though Oliver never stirred. She dismissed it as her mind playing tricks—she was exhausted, after all. Babies were hard work, even perfect ones like Oliver.

But deep down, she couldn't shake the feeling that **something was wrong.**

One cold October night, Emily was woken by the sound of **soft crying**—not the kind of cry you'd expect from a baby, but something... **older, deeper**, and filled with sorrow. It was coming from Oliver's room.

She bolted upright and rushed to the nursery. The moonlight spilled in through the window, casting long shadows across the room. Oliver lay perfectly still in his crib, but his **eyes were wide open, fixed on the doorway** as if he had been expecting her.

The crying stopped the moment Emily stepped inside.

Then, a whisper drifted through the air, faint but unmistakable:

"He's not yours."

Emily's heart raced. The air in the room grew cold, her breath coming out in visible puffs. **"Who's there?"** she whispered, scanning the shadows. But the only answer she got was the soft rustling of the wind outside.

The next morning, **Daniel found her sitting by the crib**, her face pale, her hands trembling. "Emily, what's going on? Why are you sitting here?" he asked.

She looked at him, her voice cracking. "There's something... someone... I think someone wants to take him back."

Daniel frowned. "Who? What are you talking about?"

But before Emily could explain, there was another **knock on the door**—the same soft knock she had heard when the baby first arrived.

Emily slowly opened the front door, and there, on the porch, stood **a woman**, her face pale and gaunt, her eyes sunken with exhaustion. She wore a tattered coat, and her hair clung to her damp face as though she had been wandering through the cold for days.

"I've come for him," the woman whispered, her voice brittle and sad. **"He's mine."**

Emily's heart sank. **She knew, deep down, this moment would come.** But the idea of giving Oliver away now—after finally feeling whole—was unbearable.

"You can't have him," Emily said, holding the baby close to her chest.

The woman's face crumpled with sorrow. **"Please... I didn't mean to leave him. I had no choice.** I've been looking for him... I followed him here."

Emily shook her head, her eyes filling with tears. **"He belongs with me now."**

The woman stepped closer, her eyes brimming with tears. **"No... He doesn't. And if he stays, he'll take everything from you."**

Emily felt a chill spread through her body, a dark certainty settling deep in her bones. She looked down at Oliver—those wide, innocent eyes staring back at her—and **in that moment, she saw something different.**

Something cold.

Something ancient.

Oliver's tiny mouth curled into a small smile—**a smile that didn't belong on the face of a baby.** It was the kind of smile that only something very old and very cruel could wear.

And suddenly, **Emily understood.**

This wasn't a baby. It never had been. The woman at the door wasn't here to steal Oliver. **She had been trying to warn her.**

Emily's grip tightened around Oliver as tears streamed down her face. "I love him," she whispered, her voice breaking. "He's mine."

"He will ruin you," the woman said gently, as if she had spoken these words before. **"He already has."**

Emily stood frozen, her heart breaking in two. She knew the truth. If she kept Oliver, the thing inside him would grow stronger, feeding off her love until there was nothing left of her. **He would destroy her.**

But could she give him up? Could she let him go after all the years of waiting, after finally feeling like a mother?

The woman held out her arms. "Please," she whispered. **"It's the only way to save yourself."**

With a sob, Emily kissed Oliver's cold forehead one last time. His wide eyes never blinked, never showed any sign of understanding. She pressed him into the woman's arms, her heart breaking with every second that passed.

The woman gave a small, sad smile. **"Thank you,"** she whispered, her voice filled with sorrow.

And just like that, the woman turned and walked away into the cold October night, the wind carrying her and the baby away into the darkness.

Emily stood in the doorway long after they were gone, the sound of the wind whistling through the trees. **The house felt emptier than it ever had before.**

She knew she had made the right choice. But that didn't make it any easier.

As the first snowflakes of winter drifted through the air, Emily whispered to the night: **"I hope you find peace, wherever you are."**

And for the rest of her days, every October evening, she would hear the faint sound of a baby's laugh carried by the wind, as if reminding her that **some things are not meant to stay.**

Four Steps Away

Los Angeles always felt alive—neon lights bleeding into the night, endless chatter from late-night diners, and a city that never stopped moving. But beneath the glitz and glamour, some corners of the city stayed eerily quiet. And tonight, in one such forgotten alley, the real nightmare began.

David Ford, a sound engineer by trade, had just finished a long shift at a recording studio downtown. Tired and annoyed, he decided to take a shortcut home, cutting through a back alley that split between two towering buildings. He'd done it a hundred times before. But tonight felt...off. The air was heavier, the shadows darker. The city, for once, felt silent.

As he turned the corner, he heard it—a faint, rhythmic clicking of heels behind him. Step. Step. Step. David's instincts told him someone was following, but when he glanced over his shoulder, the alley stretched empty. Just the shadows from flickering streetlights danced on the brick walls. He shook it off, thinking it was exhaustion. But the noise continued—exactly four steps behind him, always four. The footsteps stopped when he stopped. They echoed only when he moved.

His heart picked up speed. He sped up his walk, only to hear the ghostly *tap-tap-tap-tap* stay perfectly in sync, never more than four steps away. David broke into a jog, but the phantom steps followed, relentless.

Then the whispers began—soft, insidious words slithering into his ears from nowhere and everywhere. "Just four more," the voice said. David's blood ran cold. It wasn't just one voice—it was dozens, speaking in hushed tones, overlapping, like a sinister chorus.

Panic swelled inside him. He fumbled for his phone, desperate to call someone, anyone. But the screen was black, refusing to light up. No bars. No signal. It was as if the alley had swallowed him into another reality. His breath grew shallow as fear started to cloud his mind.

David turned, prepared to confront whatever was haunting him, but all he saw was... himself. Standing there, just four steps away, was a perfect reflection of him. The figure wore the same clothes, the same look of panic etched on its face—but its eyes, those eyes, were empty voids, black and soulless.

David staggered back, feeling like the air had been sucked from his lungs. The reflection smirked—a slow, sinister grin that didn't belong to him.

"Four steps, David. That's all it takes," the figure whispered, its voice a cacophony of his worst fears.

David bolted. He sprinted through the alley, his legs burning, but the steps—*tap-tap-tap-tap*—never fell behind. They stayed four paces away, no matter how fast he ran. The city blurred around him, the familiar streets twisting and contorting into an endless maze.

He could hear them—those whispers—growing louder, merging into something incomprehensible. He tried to scream, but the sound caught in his throat like a noose tightening. And then, just as he reached what felt like the end of the alley, the world stopped.

He was back at the beginning. Same alley. Same flickering lights. Same dreadful silence. But this time, something was different. His reflection wasn't four steps away anymore.

It was standing right beside him.

David's heart thundered in his chest as he stared at himself. The figure leaned in, its grin spreading wider. "You never really leave," it whispered. "Four steps away... forever."

The reflection lifted its hand and placed it gently on David's shoulder. In that moment, everything went dark—lights out, silence absolute.

The next morning, locals found an alley empty but for a single pair of shoes, perfectly placed side by side, four steps away from the nearest door.

David Ford was never seen again. But every night, if you walk through that alley and listen closely, you might hear the soft, rhythmic sound of footsteps—always four steps away. And if you ever look back...

Well, let's just say no one ever walks out of that alley twice.

Scarborough Tragedy

In the crisp autumn air of Scarborough, October winds carried the scent of damp earth and decaying leaves. The town looked picturesque, wrapped in shades of orange and gold. But there was something unsettling lurking beneath the surface—a quiet fear that spread like mist through the narrow streets, whispered from house to house. They called it *The Scarborough Tragedy*.

It began with the animals.

One by one, the pets in Scarborough started to vanish without a trace. At first, it was just the odd missing cat or an untethered dog never returning home. People shrugged it off, thinking the animals had wandered too far into the woods or met some other ordinary fate. But by mid-October, there were no animals left—not a bird chirping, not a stray cat prowling, not even the rustle of squirrels in the trees.

A silence that felt *too* heavy settled over the town.

Then came the sightings.

Old Mr. Harlow, who lived on the edge of town near the woods, swore he saw his missing Labrador, Daisy, just outside his house one evening. But Daisy didn't bark or wag her tail. She stood completely still at the edge of the garden, her black fur glistening under the cold moonlight, staring at the front door with glassy, lifeless eyes. When Harlow stepped outside, Daisy vanished into the shadows without a sound.

Soon, other townspeople reported similar sightings. Pets they had loved—dogs, cats, even caged birds—were seen briefly, standing eerily still on doorsteps, in backyards, or peeking from alleyways. They never moved, and their eyes glinted with something *otherworldly*, something *hungry*.

One family, the Fitzgeralds, had lost their tabby, Pumpkin, early in the month. One night, as little Ellie Fitzgerald slept, she woke to the familiar sound of purring. Overjoyed, she crept out of bed to find Pumpkin curled at the foot of the stairs. But something was wrong—the purring didn't sound soft and warm. It was raspy, deep, and uneven, like the dragging of claws across a chalkboard.

Ellie reached out to touch the cat, and that's when it *looked at her*. Its fur was stiff, its eyes black as obsidian, and when it opened its mouth, it let out a gurgling, human-like sigh.

"Found you..." Pumpkin whispered.

Ellie screamed, and by the time her parents reached her, there was nothing there—no Pumpkin, no sign of the thing that wore its face. Just the lingering scent of wet leaves and something rotting.

Panic gripped the town. No one knew where the animals had gone—or what they had become. But everyone knew that the sightings always preceded disaster. A week after Daisy's appearance at Harlow's door, Mr. Harlow was found in his yard—his body twisted unnaturally, his eyes wide with terror, as though he had seen something beyond comprehension in his final moments.

More tragedies followed. A woman fell from her attic window after seeing her missing parrot perched on the roof. A teenager was found drowned in the local pond, clutching the collar of the dog she had searched for all month. With each death, the animals seemed to draw closer to town, their appearances becoming more frequent, their forms *decaying* and *distorted*.

By the last week of October, the streets were deserted at night. No one dared step outside after sunset, but even indoors, the townsfolk weren't safe. Scratching noises came from inside walls, soft growls echoed from basements, and eyes—black, hollow, and patient—watched from every window.

It was on Halloween night that Scarborough fell silent once more. Not a single soul ventured out. No children knocked on doors for treats, and no lanterns flickered in windows.

And then... they came.

At midnight, the streets filled with the missing animals— silent and still, standing side by side in perfect rows, staring at the darkened houses with those empty eyes. Their bodies were mangled, some barely held together, as though stitched by invisible hands. Cats with broken spines slithered across porches; birds with no wings hopped in twisted rhythms; dogs with shattered bones limped in eerie unison.

They waited.

One by one, the doors of the town creaked open—not forced, but invited. As if the houses themselves had betrayed their occupants. From the doorways, terrified families could only watch as their once-beloved pets crossed the threshold, moving without sound, eyes gleaming with hunger.

And then, the lights in Scarborough went out.

When the sun rose the next morning, the town was empty. Not a single person remained. But the animals were still there—watching, waiting, and whispering to the autumn wind.

To this day, Scarborough lies abandoned, a ghost town where no one dares venture. But if you listen closely on a cold October night, you might hear the soft purring of a cat... or the distant howl of a dog.

And if you do, don't follow the sound.

Because not all pets come back the same.

The Horrors Follow

In the fall of 2023, a small production company in Mumbai, **Stellar Productions**, decided to make a movie. But it wasn't to win awards or entertain—it was **purely for a tax write-off**. The film wasn't meant to see the light of day. The budget was minimal, the actors inexperienced, and the story thrown together in a single night by overworked interns.

The script was titled **"The Horrors Follow"**, a vague, nonsensical plot about a cursed reel of film that haunted anyone who watched it. Filming wrapped in two weeks on a barren sound stage with terrible lighting and amateur effects. The final cut was an awkward mess—characters talking out of sync, scenes missing transitions, and sound cues misfiring at random. Stellar Productions locked the master copy away, thinking that would be the end of it.

It wasn't.

One cool October evening, a junior employee at Stellar, **Rohit**, was tasked with archiving old projects. But while uploading files to the cloud, he accidentally included **the cursed movie** in the upload.

Thinking nothing of it, he left for the night, eager to enjoy a long weekend. The next day, **The Horrors Follow** was **accidentally**

scheduled for public release on the company's streaming platform—an app with a tiny, unsuspecting user base.

By the time Stellar Productions realized the mistake, the movie had already started **streaming on screens across the country**.

And that's when the horror began.

The first reported case came from a **college student** in Bandra. He clicked on the movie, curious about its bizarre title. But halfway through the film, his phone started **glitching uncontrollably**. The screen flickered, and strange whispers began playing through the speakers—whispers that didn't belong to the film.

Just as he tried to exit the app, **the video froze**, locking the image on a distorted face—a **woman's hollow, lifeless eyes staring directly at him.** Then the whispers grew louder, filling his room with unintelligible chants. The lights flickered. His phone overheated and shut off, but the whispering continued... from **inside his room.**

The next morning, his roommate found him sitting on the floor, rocking back and forth, muttering, **"They followed me. They followed me out."**

Word spread quickly among the handful of early viewers. **Screens blacked out**, phones crashed, and devices burned hot to the touch. Some users claimed that after watching the movie, they saw **distorted figures** standing at the corners of their rooms—**shadowy figures with hollow eyes, watching... waiting.**

Soon, more chilling reports emerged. **A viewer in Thane** swore she saw the film's characters move on their own, even after the movie ended—**faces pressing against the inside of her TV screen**, as though trying to break through the glass. Another man claimed the movie kept **playing on his phone, even after he deleted the app.** And with every new sighting, the phrase repeated:

"The horrors follow."

The team at Stellar Productions scrambled to take the film offline, but every attempt failed. **The file corrupted their servers,** locking them out from removing it. Engineers reported that even unplugging the streaming system didn't work—the movie **continued playing on the platform, as if it had taken on a life of its own.**

The worst part? **It was spreading.**

People were sharing clips on social media, uploading scenes to forums, and trading copies of the movie out of morbid curiosity. No one believed the initial warnings... until it was too late. **Those who watched the movie started seeing the figures— dark shapes lurking in mirrors, reflections moving on their own, and eyes staring from the shadows.**

As the days passed, the phenomena grew worse. Some viewers disappeared without a trace, while others were found **inexplicable states of fear,** as if something **had followed them home** from the movie.

And the phrase kept repeating:

"The horrors follow."

By mid-October, panic spread through Mumbai. **Stellar Productions** was under investigation, and the public demanded answers. But no one could explain how a film—meant to be nothing more than a tax write-off—had unleashed such chaos.

Then, something even stranger happened. The file on Stellar's server **started adding new scenes**—scenes that no one had filmed. Characters the crew didn't recognize appeared in the footage—**people who had watched the film in real life**.

A scene showed a terrified man banging on a door, begging to be let in. The next shot showed him **dragged away by unseen hands** into the shadows, screaming.

And in the final scene, the distorted woman from the film stared directly into the camera, whispered, **"You brought us out. Now we'll follow you home."**

The movie cut to black.

Stellar Productions went bankrupt within weeks. The app was taken offline, but it was too late—**copies of the movie still existed, scattered across the dark corners of the internet.** People whispered about it like an urban legend, daring each other to watch it, despite knowing the risk.

And every October, new stories emerged—of people **disappearing, losing their minds, or finding strange figures standing at the foot of their beds** after watching the movie.

The final message on the movie's file remains unchanged:

"The horrors follow. Always."

And somewhere, in a dark room in Mumbai, a curious viewer presses play—unaware of the horrors waiting just beyond the screen.

Terror at the Zoo

It was the final weekend of October, and Oakwood City, Texas, was buzzing with excitement. **The Oakwood City Zoo** was hosting its first-ever **"Night Safari"**, promising guests a rare chance to see the animals after dark. Families poured in, eager for the experience, unaware that **something far more dangerous than lions or tigers** awaited them that night.

The air was crisp, with the scent of popcorn and cotton candy lingering near the entrance gates. **Leo**, a zookeeper, led one of the first groups through the dimly lit pathways. Flashlights danced across the enclosures as he explained the animals' night-time habits.

"Over there, we have our Bengal tigers," Leo said, aiming his flashlight toward the tiger enclosure. "At night, they're more alert—"

He froze. The light caught **something unusual—deep scratch marks along the inside of the glass wall.**

"Strange," Leo muttered to himself. "Maintenance must've missed that." He pushed the thought aside and continued leading the tour.

But the night only grew stranger.

As they passed the reptile house, Leo noticed that **the door to the snake exhibit was ajar.** His stomach dropped. **The exhibit housed a 20-foot-long green anaconda**, and the enclosure was supposed to remain locked at all times.

Leo shined his flashlight inside, and his worst fear was confirmed—the **anaconda was gone.**

His heart pounded as he tried to stay calm. **If the guests panicked, things would get out of hand quickly.** He radioed his colleague at the control center, but there was no response— just **static** on the other end.

"We should keep moving," Leo said, guiding the group away from the reptile house, trying to mask his growing unease. "Probably just a glitch."

But **something wasn't right**. The animals were acting strangely—the lions paced frantically, the monkeys howled incessantly, and even the usually calm elephants seemed restless. It was as if they sensed **something unnatural** in the air.

As the group moved toward the nocturnal animals exhibit, they heard **a distant scream**, sharp and panicked, coming from the direction of the staff area. Leo stiffened.

"That was... probably nothing," he muttered, though even he didn't believe it. The parents in the group exchanged uneasy glances, clutching their children a little tighter.

Suddenly, **the lights along the pathways flickered** and then went out, plunging the zoo into near-complete darkness. A low growl echoed from one of the enclosures, followed by the sound of **something heavy moving fast through the underbrush.**

Leo felt the hair on the back of his neck rise. **Something was loose.**

"We need to head back—now," he whispered urgently, guiding the group toward the exit. But as they retraced their steps, Leo noticed something chilling—**the gates to several enclosures had been unlocked.**

"What the hell…" he whispered.

A parent in the group gasped, pointing toward the trees. **Two glowing yellow eyes** stared back at them from the darkness, followed by a low, guttural snarl.

"Move!" Leo shouted. The group began to run.

They sprinted through the zoo, flashlights bouncing wildly. As they rounded a corner, they saw something that froze them in place—a massive **shadow slithered** across the path ahead. The missing anaconda.

It was **twice the size it should have been**, its body swollen and writhing unnaturally, as if **something inside it was still moving.** It hissed, and its mouth opened impossibly wide, revealing not just fangs, but **rows of human teeth**—as if **it had absorbed something… or someone.**

Suddenly, one of the children in the group screamed. From behind them, **a pack of shadowy creatures** emerged—animals, but twisted beyond recognition. The once-majestic lions now walked with their limbs bent backward, their faces elongated into something demonic. Monkeys, with **glowing red eyes**, chittered violently from the trees, their mouths stretched into unnatural grins.

"The animals... they're not right!" a mother cried.

"It's... like they're possessed!" Leo gasped, horrified by what he was seeing.

Leo led the group toward the nearest staff entrance, only to find the gate **chained shut** from the outside. **The only way out was through the main entrance**—on the other side of the zoo.

Suddenly, **the zoo's intercom crackled to life**, playing an old carnival tune. But underneath the music, they heard faint whispers, repeating the same eerie message:

"Run... or become one of us."

The group dashed forward, hearts pounding in their chests. Behind them, the monstrous animals pursued, their howls and snarls growing louder.

Leo spotted the glowing sign of the main gate in the distance. **Almost there.**

The group sprinted for the exit, with the creatures closing in fast. Leo stayed at the back, ushering everyone ahead of him, adrenaline surging through his veins.

Just as they reached the final stretch, **the massive anaconda lunged** from the bushes, its body twisting around Leo's legs. He cried out, struggling as the snake tightened its grip.

"Go!" Leo shouted to the others. "Don't stop!"

Aparna, one of the parents, hesitated, tears in her eyes, but Leo shook his head. **"Save your kids! Go!"**

The group burst through the gate, and the second they crossed the threshold, **the zoo's gates slammed shut behind them with a deafening clang.**

Panting and trembling, the survivors stood outside the gate, the zoo now eerily silent behind them. Aparna dialed emergency services, but when the operator answered, her voice was cold and detached:

"There is no Oakwood City Zoo. It closed down... years ago."

The group stared at the towering gates in disbelief. Behind the bars, the shadows shifted, and **a pair of glowing yellow eyes** watched them from the darkness.

And then... the whispers returned, drifting through the cool October night:

"You escaped... but not for long. The zoo always calls you back."

As the survivors turned to leave, one of the children tugged on Aparna's sleeve, pointing at the road ahead.

"Mom... where did Leo go?"

But **Leo was gone**—and somewhere, deep inside the zoo, **a new creature slithered through the darkness**, with familiar, terrified eyes.

The Sorrow Follows

•❖•

October 28th, deep in the heart of **Alabama**, the air carried a weight of sorrow—like a heavy fog that settled over the town of **Ravenshollow**, a place where the past always seemed just one step behind the present. Some said the land was cursed, that it carried the remnants of something ancient and angry. Others believed that **grief had taken root**, growing wild among the people like vines that could never be cut back.

On this day, a **storm was brewing**—not just in the sky, but in the lives of the people of Ravenshollow. And at the center of it all was **Anna Gracefield**, a woman haunted by the memory of her son, who had vanished a year ago to the day.

The night **her son Thomas disappeared** had been cold and rainy, much like tonight. One minute he was playing outside with his dog by the old **oak tree**, and the next, he was gone. No footprints, no sounds—just **silence and an empty yard**.

For twelve months, Anna had searched every corner of the town, but **no answers ever came**. The police told her to move on. The neighbors avoided her, fearing her grief was **contagious**. Even her husband, **David**, grew distant, as if pretending Thomas had never existed would ease the pain. But Anna knew better. She could **feel Thomas, just out of reach**, like a shadow at the corner of her vision.

And now, on the eve of **October 28th**, something was calling her—something she could no longer ignore.

That night, as the storm rolled in, **Anna found herself drawn to the oak tree**. The rain began to fall in heavy sheets, but she didn't care. She felt a pull, stronger than fear, stronger than reason—a whisper carried on the wind that **sounded like Thomas's voice**.

"**Mama... I'm waiting.**"

Her heart pounded in her chest as she stepped through the yard, the wind howling around her. The oak tree swayed in the storm, **its branches creaking like old bones**. And beneath it, where Thomas used to play, lay **a single red balloon**, tied to a broken swing.

She stared at the balloon, her breath hitching in her throat. **This wasn't possible.**

And then, the balloon **twitched**, as if something unseen had nudged it.

Before Anna could turn away, the wind seemed to **shift**. It no longer carried the scent of rain, but **something older, colder**—like the breath of an open grave. She looked up into the branches of the oak, and for a moment, she saw them—**figures swaying** between the limbs, their pale faces turned toward her.

Their eyes were empty sockets, their mouths slightly open, as if frozen mid-scream. And at the center of them, among the tangled branches, hung a boy in a tattered red jacket—**Thomas**.

"No..." Anna whispered, stumbling backward. **"This can't be real."**

But the boy's head turned slowly, the creak of the rope blending with the wind. **"Mama,"** he whispered, his voice faint and brittle. **"You were supposed to find me."**

Anna's knees gave out, and she fell to the ground, sobbing. "I tried, baby," she whispered. **"I never stopped looking."**

The boy's gaze softened for a moment, as if he understood. But then, the other children began to stir, their **shadows lengthening** across the wet grass. They whispered in unison, a soft chorus of sorrow and regret:

"You're too late. The sorrow follows."

Anna tried to get up, but **her limbs felt heavy,** as if the very ground was pulling her down. The shadows twisted around her like creeping vines, **wrapping around her wrists and ankles,** dragging her deeper into the wet earth.

She screamed, but the sound was swallowed by the storm.

When the storm cleared the next morning, David went outside, calling for Anna. But **she was nowhere to be found.** The only thing left beneath the oak tree was the old, broken swing—**and a single red balloon, bobbing gently in the breeze.**

The neighbors whispered about Anna's disappearance, but no one searched for her. **They all knew the truth,** though none dared say it aloud:

The sorrow had taken her, just as it had taken Thomas. **And once sorrow finds you, it never lets go.**

Every October 28th, the storm returns to Ravenshollow, and people swear they can hear **the voices of lost children** whispering on the wind, calling for their mothers, begging to be found. **Balloons** appear in unexpected places—tied to fences, caught in branches, or floating aimlessly down empty streets.

And if you listen closely, just as the clock strikes midnight, you might hear it:

The soft creak of a swing.

And if you do—**don't look.** Because if you see the children swaying from the branches, it means the sorrow has chosen you next.

And once **the sorrow follows...** it never lets go.

Part II:
Curses & Rituals

The Sun Forest

Deep in the **Amazonian jungles of Peru**, there exists a place whispered about among locals—**The Sun Forest**. They say it's a stretch of dense jungle where sunlight pierces through the canopy at odd angles, and where the **sun itself seems alive**. It's a place that promises beauty and wonder—but those who venture too far into it never come back the same, if they come back at all. **October** was the worst time to visit, the elders warned, for that's when the forest awakened.

And yet, **Elias Vasquez,** a seasoned anthropologist, found himself standing at the edge of the Sun Forest on the eve of **October 30th**, drawn in by stories of **ancient Incan relics hidden deep within**—artifacts untouched for centuries. The sun dipped low, casting strange golden beams through the twisted branches, and Elias knew he had no choice but to **go deeper**.

The Sun Forest welcomed Elias with **an unsettling beauty**. The trees shimmered with light, their leaves glowing faintly in the soft sunbeams. Birds chirped, and the wind rustled through the canopy, but something about the sounds felt... off. As if **the forest was imitating life**, rather than truly living it.

Elias checked his compass. **The needle spun wildly,** unable to find true north. He shook it and tried again—still nothing. The forest was **warping space** around him, but he dismissed the thought as nonsense. **Superstition had no place in science.**

And yet, there it was—a faint **hum in the air**, like distant chanting carried on the wind. Elias squinted through the dense foliage and saw it: **a golden glimmer** deep within the forest.

The deeper Elias ventured, the brighter the forest became. The sunlight no longer came from above—it seemed to **radiate from within the trees themselves**, as if the forest was its own source of light. His skin tingled with warmth, and his heart raced as the chanting grew louder, echoing from unseen places.

He stumbled upon **carvings in the bark of the trees—Incan symbols**—marking the way forward. They told a story of **a sun god**—one who **devoured those who sought his light**, binding their souls to the forest for eternity. Elias felt a shiver crawl down his spine but pressed on, curiosity overtaking fear.

Finally, he arrived at **a clearing**, and in the center stood **an ancient altar**, bathed in golden light. Atop the altar rested a small **idol**, carved from stone and gold, shaped like a blazing sun. **The Sun Idol.**

Elias smiled. **He had found it.**

As Elias reached for the idol, the forest seemed to **exhale**—a long, low breath that **shifted the air around him**. The golden light, once warm and inviting, turned harsh and searing.

And that's when he realized: **the forest had been waiting for him.**

The chanting grew louder, deafening, as **the trees bent toward him**, their leaves shimmering with unnatural light. **The beams of sunlight wrapped around his arms, pulling him closer to the altar.**

He tried to let go of the idol, but his hands wouldn't obey. His fingers clung to the stone, as if **the forest had taken control** of his body. The light twisted and turned, curling around him like vines, tightening with every second.

Elias screamed, but his voice was **swallowed by the forest.**

The golden beams pierced through his skin, burning his veins with light. He felt himself **being pulled apart**, his mind unraveling as the chanting turned into laughter—a cruel, ancient sound, like **the sun itself mocking him.**

And then, **the light consumed him.**

His body dissolved into the beams, his flesh becoming part of the radiance that filled the forest. His soul stretched thin, woven into the light that flickered through the leaves. **He was no longer Elias Vasquez.** He was **part of the forest now**, another whisper in the endless glow.

The Sun Forest **had taken what it was owed.**

Weeks later, **a search party arrived** at the edge of the Sun Forest, following the faint traces of Elias's path. They found **his backpack, untouched**, and his compass—**the needle still spinning aimlessly.**

But there was no sign of Elias.

As the search team stood in the clearing, **the sunlight pierced through the trees**, bathing them in golden warmth. One of the men stepped closer to the altar, mesmerized by the glow.

And as he reached out toward the idol, **the forest sighed**, and the light shifted once more.

Because in the Sun Forest, **the morning always belongs to the light**. And those who enter **never leave—at least, not as themselves.**

The Vacation

October in Salem, Massachusetts, was nothing short of magical—or so Ben and Jessica had thought when they booked their stay. The couple, tired of their dull routine in New York, wanted a little adventure: ghost tours, Halloween festivities, and crisp autumn air. It was the perfect getaway.

Their vacation rental, an old colonial house on the outskirts of town, looked picture-perfect online. "It's authentic!" Jessica had said, excited about the charm of staying somewhere with real history. The property owner had even mentioned it was over 300 years old, with a distant connection to the Salem witch trials.

But from the moment they arrived, things felt off. The key was left under the mat, as promised, but the air inside the house was stale, as if it hadn't been opened to visitors in years.

"Smells... old," Ben muttered, setting their bags down.

Jessica brushed it off. "It's supposed to smell old, Ben. That's the point."

The house was dimly lit by oil lamps, though they had no idea why. It felt unsettling, as if the light struggled to keep the darkness at bay. They toured the house together: creaky floorboards, low-beamed ceilings, and furniture that looked like it belonged in a museum.

"Authentic, huh?" Ben said, trying to shake the chill creeping up his spine.

"Come on, it's cozy," Jessica insisted, though her voice wavered. "Let's just settle in."

They opened some wine, turned on some music, and tried to make the place feel like a home. But no matter what they did, the house remained eerily silent between songs, as if waiting for something. Outside, the forest pressed in on the windows, thick with shadows. They couldn't see another house or person for miles.

That night, they settled into the bed—an antique four-poster that groaned under their weight—and drifted off to sleep. Or at least, Jessica did.

Ben woke at 2:34 a.m., heart pounding in his chest. The room felt... wrong. The kind of wrong that makes your skin crawl before you even know why. He glanced at Jessica beside him, sound asleep, and then noticed something strange: **the door to the bedroom was wide open**.

He was sure they had closed it.

A chill slid down his spine, and he got out of bed quietly, padding to the doorway to shut it. But as he reached the threshold, he froze. **Footsteps echoed from the staircase below**—slow, deliberate, and heavy.

Ben's breath hitched. "Jessica…" he whispered, shaking her shoulder. She stirred but didn't wake fully.

He strained his ears. The footsteps had stopped… but the feeling of being watched didn't. His hand hovered over the door handle when, suddenly, **it slammed shut on its own**, nearly taking his fingers off.

Ben stumbled backward, gasping. "Jess! Jess, wake up!"

Jessica bolted upright, eyes wide with confusion. "What? What's wrong?"

"The door—it… it shut by itself," Ben stammered, his pulse racing.

Jessica blinked groggily. "Ben, you're scaring me."

"I'm scaring *you*? Someone's in the house!" he hissed. But as they sat in tense silence, the air around them seemed to grow heavier, pressing down on their chests like a weight.

And then, they heard it: **a soft humming**—a woman's voice, faint and melodic, drifting up the stairs like a lullaby from another world.

Jessica clutched Ben's arm. "That's coming from inside the house."

The humming grew louder, more insistent. It wasn't a song they recognized. It was slow, mournful, like a dirge for someone long gone. And beneath the melody, they could hear whispers… in a language they couldn't understand.

Ben grabbed Jessica's hand. "We're leaving. Now."

They stumbled down the staircase, the humming following them like a shadow. As they reached the front door, Jessica screamed. **The door wouldn't open.** No matter how hard they pulled or yanked, the handle wouldn't budge.

And then they noticed it—something that hadn't been there when they arrived.

A dusty, cracked mirror hung on the wall near the door, and in its glass, they saw something that made their blood run cold.

Their reflections stood frozen, eyes black as night, mouths stitched shut with thin, rotting thread. **The things in the mirror smiled at them.**

Jessica's voice cracked. "Ben… what is that?"

The figures in the mirror moved, even though neither Ben nor Jessica had shifted. Their doppelgängers reached forward, pressing their hands against the inside of the glass. The surface shimmered like water, rippling as their mirrored selves began **clawing their way out.**

Ben yanked Jessica back just as the first pale hand broke through the mirror's surface. "Run!" he shouted, dragging her toward the kitchen.

The humming followed them, louder now—angrier. The walls seemed to pulse with the rhythm of it, and the house twisted around them like a maze. Hallways stretched impossibly long, doors led nowhere, and the windows showed nothing but swirling darkness.

"Where's the exit?!" Jessica cried, panic setting in.

Ben didn't answer—he couldn't. He didn't know. The house had shifted, trapping them inside like flies in a web. Every door they opened revealed more darkness... or **the figures from the mirror, waiting with stitched mouths and hollow eyes**.

Finally, they found a back door leading into the forest. Ben shoved it open, and the two of them bolted into the cold night air. They ran through the woods, their breath visible in the moonlight, branches clawing at their clothes and faces. The house behind them seemed to groan in disappointment, the humming fading into the distance as they escaped.

They didn't stop running until they reached the car, parked at the edge of the property. Ben fumbled with the keys, hands shaking, and the engine roared to life.

"Drive!" Jessica screamed, and Ben slammed on the gas.

They sped down the road, the forest thinning around them. Relief washed over them as they left the cursed house behind— until Jessica glanced into the rearview mirror.

Her heart stopped.

In the backseat, barely visible in the dim light, **sat their reflections**—smiling with blackened eyes, mouths stitched shut.

And then, the humming began again.

The Sorrow Follows Her

New Alabama, a newly developed town on the edge of swampland, looked pristine on the surface—new houses with fresh paint, clean streets, and families eager for a fresh start. But something dark lurked beneath its polished facade. **October** brought not just chilly winds but strange, unexplainable things. People whispered about strange sightings—**red balloons drifting silently** at night, children's voices heard on the wind, and swings that swayed without anyone near them.

At the center of these whispered rumors was the **Gracefield house**, which sat abandoned on the outskirts of town, its windows boarded up and its yard overgrown. No one dared go near it, not since Anna Gracefield and her son vanished **a year ago in Ravenshollow**. But now, in New Alabama, something—or someone—was waiting.

It was the night of **October 28th** when **Claire Holloway**, a young reporter new to the town, received a strange tip. **"They say Anna Gracefield is back,"** the voice on the other end whispered. **"She's come here."**

Claire had heard the story—the woman whose son went missing, only for her to disappear beneath the old oak tree in Ravenshollow. Curious and with a sense of foreboding, Claire decided to investigate. She grabbed her camera and headed toward the edge of town, toward the old Gracefield house.

As she approached the house, the wind **picked up**, and the first drops of rain began to fall. **A red balloon floated lazily** from behind the trees, bobbing toward her on the wind. Claire stopped in her tracks, her heart racing.

When the balloon passed, **she saw her—a woman standing at the front steps, soaked in rain, her clothes tattered and her eyes hollow.** It was Anna Gracefield.

"I need your help," Anna whispered, her voice barely audible over the wind. **"It's not over."**

Claire's breath caught in her throat. **"You disappeared—how are you here?"**

Anna's pale face twisted into a pained expression. **"They followed me. I tried to leave them behind, but the sorrow— it follows. It always follows."** She looked up at Claire with desperate eyes. **"You have to help me stop it."**

Before Claire could respond, the rain came down harder, and **the distant sound of children's laughter echoed through the trees.** Anna turned toward the sound, her eyes wide with fear.

"They're here."

Claire followed Anna into the house just as **a heavy fog rolled over the yard**, swallowing the world in white mist. Inside, the air was cold, and the walls seemed to pulse with an unseen energy.

"We have to end it here, tonight," Anna said, pacing the room. **"If we don't, they'll take more."**

"Who?" Claire asked, her voice trembling.

Anna stopped and looked at her with haunted eyes. **"The children. The ones lost to the sorrow. They come for others—they need more souls to escape."**

The sound of **footsteps pattering on the porch** made Claire's blood run cold. She turned to the window just in time to see **shadowy figures** moving through the fog—small, childlike forms, their faces twisted in silent screams.

And then she saw it: **a red balloon floating toward the house,** carried by invisible hands.

Anna moved quickly, grabbing an old journal from the mantel. **"We have to trap them. They can't leave this place."**

Before Claire could ask how, the front door **burst open**, and the children stepped inside—**pale figures**, dripping with water, their faces sunken and their eyes glowing with a dim, unnatural light.

One of the children—the smallest—**reached out to Anna,** his cracked lips forming a single word: **"Mama."**

Anna collapsed to her knees, tears streaming down her face. **It was Thomas.**

Thomas's outstretched hand trembled as if he were torn between two worlds. Anna knew what she had to do. **"I'm sorry, baby,"** she whispered, clutching his tiny hand. **"I should have found you sooner."**

She turned to Claire, her voice resolute. **"Get out. Now. They need me—only me."**

Claire shook her head. **"I'm not leaving you."**

"You have to!" Anna cried. **"If you stay, the sorrow will take you too."**

The children moved closer, their **eyes glowing brighter**, the fog swirling around them like a living thing. Anna stood and gave Claire a look of fierce determination. **"I'll hold them here. But you have to leave—and never come back."**

Claire stumbled out of the house, the fog pressing against her like a weight. As she reached the edge of the yard, she looked back one last time.

Anna stood in the doorway, **surrounded by the ghostly children**, her face calm and at peace for the first time in years. She gave Claire a small, sad smile before the door **slammed shut**, sealing the house and everything inside it.

And then, just like that, the **fog lifted**. The red balloon popped with a soft hiss, and the house **went silent**.

By the next morning, the **Gracefield house was gone**—as if it had never existed. The land where it stood was **an empty lot**, overgrown with weeds and scattered with fallen leaves.

But the people of New Alabama knew better. Every **October 28th**, the wind would carry strange sounds through the town— **children's voices, the creak of a swing, and the faint pop of a red balloon.**

And those who heard the whispers knew to stay indoors— because once sorrow follows, **it never lets go.**

The Sun Fortress

The **jungles of Borneo** are known for their ancient trees, humid air, and the mysteries that lurk beneath the thick canopy. Hidden deep within this remote wilderness lies something far stranger than the wildlife and rare plants—**a structure whispered about only in hushed tones** by local tribes: **The Sun Fortress.**

The fortress wasn't on any map, and few dared to speak its name aloud. The legend claimed that **it was built by the same forces that created the Sun Forest**, far away in Peru—**two realms connected by something older than civilization itself.** But no one knew how or why they were linked.

And yet, on **October 14th**, a research team led by **Dr. Rowan Ellis** stumbled upon **its overgrown entrance**, unaware that **their discovery would awaken something ancient and vengeful.**

Dr. Ellis wasn't searching for legends—**she was after ancient artifacts.** Her team had been tracking traces of **a forgotten tribe** that lived in the Bornean jungle centuries ago. The deeper they ventured into the dense forest, the more strange symbols they found—**sun shapes carved into stones**, similar to those found in distant cultures halfway across the world.

And then they found it: **The Sun Fortress.**

It was a massive structure, partially collapsed and swallowed by vines, **its walls glowing faintly** as if absorbing the sunlight from above. The fortress was built into the mountainside, with **ancient stone doors covered in carvings of swirling suns.**

"We've found something incredible," Dr. Ellis whispered, awestruck. But as they pushed the doors open, they felt a cold wind sweep through the jungle—**a warning, perhaps, or a curse.**

Inside, the air was dry, the walls covered in ancient glyphs that depicted **a sun deity surrounded by writhing figures**, their faces twisted in agony. The beams of sunlight that managed to pierce through the cracks in the ceiling **moved unnaturally—** as if alive, shifting with every step the team took.

The deeper they ventured, the brighter the light became, **reflecting off the golden surfaces embedded in the walls.** Strange artifacts lay scattered across the stone floor—**mirrors, obsidian stones**, and what looked like **ancient lenses**, as if the entire fortress had been built to harness and manipulate light itself.

And at the heart of the fortress lay **a massive altar**, much like the one in the Sun Forest—but far more elaborate. **A golden sphere sat atop the altar**, radiating warmth.

The team didn't realize it at the time, but **the fortress wasn't abandoned**. It had simply been waiting.

As soon as Dr. Ellis touched the golden sphere, **the entire fortress shuddered**, as though it had taken a breath after centuries of stillness. **The light inside the walls twisted violently**, beams shooting in every direction.

Suddenly, the jungle outside darkened—**as if the sun had been stolen from the sky**. The team's lanterns flickered, casting wild shadows on the walls. The beams of light shifted, curling like serpents, **encircling the researchers one by one.**

"Get out!" Rowan shouted, but it was too late.

The walls began to hum, and the figures carved into the stone seemed to writhe to life. Shadows stretched and elongated, their forms taking shape—**people trapped between realms, bound to the fortress and consumed by the light.**

The legend was true. **The Sun Fortress wasn't just a structure—it was a prison.** Those who entered became part of the light, their souls devoured by the very thing they sought to understand.

The beams wrapped around Rowan's colleagues, **dragging them into the walls**. Their screams echoed through the chambers, turning into eerie whispers as they were absorbed into the light. Their faces appeared within the golden surface of the sphere, their eyes hollow and lifeless.

Rowan could feel the warmth of the light **creeping toward her**—an ancient hunger that demanded her essence. But as she stumbled backward, her hand brushed against a glyph carved into the stone—a symbol that glowed faintly under her touch.

Suddenly, she understood: **The Sun Fortress wasn't just connected to the Sun Forest—it was a mirror.** Whatever power had been awakened in Peru had now spread here, and it was **unstoppable**.

Rowan ran through the twisting corridors, the fortress shifting and closing behind her, as if trying to trap her within. **The light followed**, relentless and merciless, burning everything in its path. She could hear the whispers of her lost colleagues, calling out to her from the walls:

"Stay with us... The light is beautiful..."

The entrance was just ahead. Rowan sprinted toward it as **the golden beams licked at her heels**, the air around her growing hotter and thicker with every step. Just as she reached the threshold, **the doors slammed shut behind her**, and the light vanished—trapped inside the fortress once more.

Gasping for breath, Rowan collapsed on the forest floor, her skin still warm from the touch of the ancient light. **The fortress had let her go—but not without leaving its mark.**

Rowan stumbled back to the nearest village, **haunted by the whispers** that followed her from the fortress. No one believed her story—no one ever did. But she could feel it: **the light had touched her**, and it would never truly let her go.

As she lay awake that night, staring at the ceiling of her small hut, she saw it—**a faint beam of golden light** creeping through the window, curling toward her like a hungry serpent.

The light had found her.

And **it would never stop searching.**

The Shaman

October in Kentucky was colder than usual. The leaves had turned the color of fire, and the air carried the sharp bite of the coming winter. But the chill that haunted Callie Stevens wasn't from the cold. It was from **the dreams**—horrifying, vivid dreams that had plagued her every night for weeks.

In these dreams, Callie found herself trapped in a strange forest, a place where the trees bled and shadows whispered her name. Something was always watching, lurking just beyond sight— something ancient and malevolent. Each time she tried to wake up, **she would find herself back in the same dream**, deeper in the nightmare, as if her mind refused to let her escape.

It began small—a feeling of being watched, hearing footsteps behind her that weren't there. But soon, the dreams bled into reality. Strange scratches appeared on her arms, claw marks she had no memory of getting. Lights flickered in her apartment, and she could swear she heard whispering in the dead of night, even when she was wide awake.

Desperate and exhausted, Callie confided in her closest friend, Sarah.

"I can't take it anymore," Callie said over coffee, her hands trembling. "It's like I'm being hunted in my own head. I don't know what's real or what's a dream."

Sarah leaned in closer, lowering her voice. "I know someone who might help."

"Who?" Callie asked, her voice shaky with both hope and skepticism.

"There's a shaman," Sarah whispered. "He's not exactly... conventional, but I've heard things. People say he can deal with stuff like this. Curses, spirits... nightmares."

"A shaman?" Callie frowned. "Come on, Sarah, that sounds ridiculous."

Sarah shrugged. "What's ridiculous is living like this, barely sleeping, thinking you're going crazy. Just meet him. What do you have to lose?"

Reluctantly, Callie agreed.

The next day, Callie drove deep into the backwoods of Kentucky, where GPS signals faltered, and roads twisted like veins through the dense forest. She followed Sarah's directions to a rundown cabin at the edge of an overgrown field. The air was thick with the smell of damp earth and old wood, and the forest loomed around the cabin like a hungry predator waiting to pounce.

The man who answered the door didn't look like what Callie had expected. He was old, but not frail. His sharp blue eyes seemed to see through her, reading everything she tried to hide. He introduced himself only as **Silas**.

"You've been having dreams," Silas said before she could even speak.

Callie shivered. "How... how did you know?"

"They've been calling to you," he answered cryptically, stepping aside to let her in. "And now they've found you."

The cabin's interior was filled with strange artifacts—animal bones, jars of herbs, and symbols carved into the walls. The air inside was heavy, as if the walls held memories far older than they should.

Silas motioned for her to sit. "Tell me everything."

Callie told him about the dreams—the forest, the bleeding trees, the whispers, the scratches on her arms. As she spoke, Silas listened in silence, his expression unreadable.

When she finished, he leaned forward, his voice low. "What's chasing you in the dream isn't a figment of your imagination. It's **real**."

Callie felt her stomach drop. "What do you mean, real?"

"There are things that live in places we don't understand—spirits that slip through cracks in reality. Some are drawn to fear, others to regret. And some... are drawn to dreams. You've caught the attention of something that feeds on your terror. It won't stop until it's consumed you."

The words felt like ice running through her veins. "What do I do?"

Silas stood and gathered a bundle of herbs, a clay bowl, and a knife. "We need to perform a ritual. Tonight."

As night fell, the forest outside seemed to come alive, pressing against the windows of the cabin. Silas built a fire in the center of the room, chanting under his breath in a language Callie didn't recognize. He handed her the knife.

"You'll have to open yourself to the spirit," Silas said. "Offer it a piece of yourself—but just enough to lure it out. No more."

Callie stared at the blade, her hands trembling. "What happens if I mess up?"

Silas didn't answer, but the look in his eyes was enough to tell her that failure wasn't an option.

She made a shallow cut on her palm, wincing as the blood welled up. The moment the first drop hit the clay bowl, **the air changed**. The fire flickered wildly, and the shadows on the walls twisted into grotesque shapes.

Then came the whisper—a voice she knew too well, the same voice from her dreams. **It was inside the room with them.**

"You can't escape," the voice hissed, sounding like a chorus of a thousand overlapping whispers. "You belong to us."

The room grew colder. The fire dimmed. And from the shadows emerged a figure—a shape half-formed, flickering between human and beast. Its eyes glowed a sickly yellow, and its mouth twisted into a grin too wide for its face.

Silas began chanting louder, throwing herbs into the fire. The flames roared to life, and the creature recoiled, hissing in fury. But it didn't retreat. Instead, it lunged toward Callie.

She felt it in her mind—a sharp, unbearable pressure, like claws digging into her thoughts. **It was trying to pull her back into the dream, to trap her forever.**

"Fight it!" Silas shouted. "It's feeding on your fear—don't let it win!"

Callie clenched her fists, her heart pounding in her chest. The thing's grip tightened, dragging her toward the abyss of her own mind.

Then, somewhere deep inside, **Callie found something stronger than fear**—anger. Pure, burning rage at the thing that had tormented her, stolen her peace, and made her feel helpless.

With a scream, she pushed back against the creature, shattering its grip. The shadow let out a deafening screech as the fire roared higher, consuming it in a blaze of light.

And then... silence.

The fire crackled softly. The cabin was still. The creature was gone.

Silas nodded approvingly. "You did it."

Callie collapsed to the floor, gasping for breath. "Is it... is it over?"

"For now," Silas said. "But these things don't give up easily. It'll try to find its way back to you. But next time... you'll be ready."

Callie left the cabin just before dawn, the first light of the new day cutting through the misty forest. As she drove back toward town, she felt lighter, as if a weight had been lifted from her soul.

But as she glanced in the rearview mirror, her heart skipped a beat.

For just a moment—barely a flicker—she saw it again. **The shadow**, sitting in the backseat, grinning with glowing yellow eyes.

It was still with her.

The Bard's Sorrow

The winds that swept through the **Sahara Desert** in **Algeria** carried ancient stories—tales of **lost love, cursed promises, and haunting melodies** that were never meant to be heard by mortal ears. And every **October**, when the desert nights grew colder and longer, one such story resurfaced—a tale known among villagers as **The Bard's Sorrow.** It was a song, they whispered, that could unravel the heart of anyone who dared listen to it in full.

No one knew where the song came from, but it was said to belong to a **traveling bard**, who had once wandered through the desert villages. He played music so beautiful that it could make even the **harsh desert bloom with flowers**. But one day, **the bard fell in love with a woman** who belonged to another, and when his love went unanswered, he played **a final, sorrowful melody** beneath her window—a song so powerful that it **changed the course of his soul.**

That was the night **the bard vanished**, leaving behind nothing but his instrument—**a lute** said to be cursed, for no one who touched it would ever live without hearing the bard's sorrow in their dreams.

It was **October 18th** when **Youssef Benali**, an amateur musician from Algiers, stumbled upon **an old, dusty lute** in a curio shop tucked deep within the city's marketplace. The shop owner had been reluctant to sell it, murmuring something about **ancient curses**, but Youssef dismissed it. After all, **a story was just a story**, and the instrument itself was exquisite—made of aged cedar, the wood darkened with time, and strings that sang even when touched lightly.

"This will be perfect," Youssef thought. **He had a performance to prepare**—a festival set to take place under the stars in the village of Ghardaïa. He didn't believe in curses or bards who vanished into thin air. **Music was music**, nothing more.

But from the moment he placed his fingers on the lute that night, **something stirred in the air**—something ancient and sorrowful. He played a few notes, and **the melody slipped from his fingers**, smooth and haunting, as if it had been waiting for him to release it. The notes seemed to **come alive**, wrapping around him, sinking into his mind like roots burrowing deep into soil.

And that night, Youssef dreamed.

In his dream, Youssef found himself standing **in a vast, endless desert**, beneath a sky heavy with stars. **A figure stood before him**—a man dressed in tattered robes, holding a lute identical to the one Youssef had just purchased.

The man's face was hidden beneath a hood, but **his eyes glowed with sorrow**, and his voice echoed through the empty expanse:

"You've played my song... Now you must finish it."

Youssef woke with a start, his heart pounding. **The melody lingered in his mind**, as vivid as if he had just played it. The air in his room felt heavy, and a strange chill spread through the small apartment, despite the warmth of the Algerian night.

But the strangest part was that the lute—**the very one from the shop**—sat at the edge of his bed, though he had left it in the other room.

Despite the strange dream, Youssef traveled to Ghardaïa as planned. The festival was in full swing, the scent of grilled lamb and sweet mint tea filling the night air. **Musicians and poets performed beneath the stars**, their sounds blending with the murmurs of the desert breeze.

When Youssef's turn came, he stepped onto the makeshift stage, the lute cradled in his hands. The villagers sat silently, waiting for him to begin. And as soon as his fingers touched the strings, **the melody returned**—the same sorrowful tune from his dream, unfolding effortlessly from his hands.

The crowd listened, entranced. But something strange began to happen—**the stars above them flickered**, and the wind died down completely, leaving the night eerily still. The longer Youssef played, **the heavier the air became**, as if the very fabric of the night was folding in on itself.

And then, **the voice came.**

It began as a low hum, rising from the windless desert—**the voice of the bard**. It carried sorrow and regret, growing louder with every note Youssef played.

"You've summoned me," the voice whispered, cutting through the melody like a knife. **"And now you must take my place."**

The villagers gasped as **a figure appeared at the edge of the crowd**—a man in tattered robes, his face hidden beneath a hood, holding an identical lute. **It was the bard.** His presence was heavy, as if the weight of centuries hung around him, and **his hollow eyes locked onto Youssef.**

"Finish the song," the bard whispered. **"Or the sorrow will never leave you."**

Youssef's hands trembled, but he couldn't stop playing—the melody had taken control, **guiding his fingers** like a marionette on strings. **The crowd sat frozen**, trapped in the spell of the song, unable to move or speak.

The bard stepped closer, **his hollow eyes glowing brighter**, and Youssef knew that if he finished the song, **his soul would be claimed**—just as the bard's had been, centuries ago.

But if he stopped... **the curse would spread**, and the sorrow would take hold of everyone who had heard even a single note.

With tears streaming down his face, **Youssef made his choice.**

He strummed the final note, and as the sound echoed through the desert night, **the bard smiled—a smile filled with sorrow and relief.** His form dissolved into the wind, and **the stars above flickered back to life.**

The crowd stirred, blinking as if waking from a dream, unaware of the terror that had nearly consumed them.

When the festival ended and the villagers returned to their homes, **Youssef remained alone on the stage**, the lute heavy in his hands. **He had finished the song—but at a cost.** The bard was gone, but the curse lived on, buried deep within the strings of the lute.

And from that day forward, **Youssef could never stop playing.** Every night, the melody returned to him, dragging him back into the endless sorrow that **the bard had left behind.**

He became a wanderer, **roaming from village to village,** playing the cursed song beneath the stars—just as the bard before him had done.

And the people whispered of a **sorrowful musician**, whose music could break your heart and bind your soul if you listened too closely.

Because in the desert nights of Algeria, **the bard's sorrow never truly ends.**

It's in the Blood

The halls of **St. Mary's Hospital** in Memphis were unusually quiet that October night. The building creaked under the weight of the midnight air, and the fluorescent lights flickered overhead, casting strange shadows across the sterile white walls. It was the kind of night when even seasoned nurses felt uneasy, as if **something unseen** was stalking just beyond the edges of the light.

Down in the **basement lab**, a young technician named **Theo Grant** yawned as he sat at his desk, waiting for the latest batch of blood samples to finish processing. **He hated the night shift**, but tonight felt worse than usual. The air in the basement was thick and cold, as if the walls themselves were holding their breath.

Theo glanced at the time—**2:13 a.m.** The hospital was dead quiet, except for the low hum of machines and the occasional groan of the building settling. He checked the labels on the samples lined up on the counter—**routine tests**, mostly.

Except one.

A **small vial**, sealed tighter than the others, with **no name**—just a strange sequence of numbers scrawled across the label: **0013-X**.

Theo frowned. He didn't remember seeing it before. And something about the dark, **viscous blood inside** made his skin crawl.

Curious, Theo scanned the sample into the system. But as soon as he did, **the screen glitched**—the usual green interface flickered, replaced by **rows of strange symbols** that looked like jagged spirals and slashes.

"What the hell?" Theo muttered, tapping the keyboard. But the screen froze, the strange symbols dancing across it like static. Then, just as quickly, the system rebooted, showing the usual data.

But something was wrong.

The blood sample had come back flagged as **anomalous**—the system reporting **unknown proteins** and **unidentifiable cells** that didn't match anything in the hospital's database. **The cells were still alive**, the readout said. **And they were multiplying.**

Theo stared at the screen, a cold knot forming in his stomach. **This was no ordinary blood sample.**

Then the lights overhead flickered—and **went out**.

Theo grabbed his phone, flicking on the flashlight. **The basement was plunged into darkness**, the hum of machines fading to a deafening silence. He stood still, listening to the drip of water from an unseen pipe, trying to shake the feeling that he wasn't alone.

And then he heard it—**a soft, wet sound**.

It was coming from the counter where the vial sat. Slowly, Theo turned the light toward it—and his heart stopped.

The vial had cracked open. **The dark blood was spreading** across the surface of the counter, slithering like it had a mind of its own. Tiny tendrils reached out, curling and stretching, **as if the blood were searching for something.**

Theo backed away, heart pounding in his chest. He fumbled for his radio. "This is Grant, down in the lab... we have a situation. I need security and—"

The radio **hissed with static**. And then, beneath the crackle, he heard a voice—**his own voice**—whispering:

"It's in the blood, Theo."

Panic surged through him. He turned toward the exit, but the hallway was **pitch black**—the emergency lights hadn't kicked in. He could feel the cold air pressing in, thick and heavy, as if **something was crawling beneath his skin.**

And then he saw it: **a figure standing at the far end of the hallway**, its eyes gleaming in the dark.

Theo shined his light toward it—and **the figure twitched**. It was a **nurse**, or at least it had been. Her skin was pale, her eyes sunken and empty, and her veins stood out beneath her skin—**black as ink**, pulsing with every beat of her heart.

"The blood," she whispered, her voice thin and broken. "**It's hungry.**"

Before Theo could react, the nurse lunged forward, her limbs bending in unnatural ways, **her mouth stretched wide into a grotesque grin**.

Theo bolted down the hall, his shoes slapping against the cold tiles. Behind him, **the infected nurse crawled after him**, her bones cracking as she scuttled along the floor like a spider.

He reached the stairwell and slammed the door behind him, his breath ragged. But as he leaned against the door, **something warm dripped onto his hand**.

He looked down—and saw it.

A thin line of black veins had appeared under his skin, slowly spreading from the tips of his fingers. **It was inside him.**

"No," Theo whispered, panic rising in his throat. He needed help—**now**.

He stumbled up the stairs and burst through the doors into the emergency ward. The lights flickered overhead, but at least there were people—**doctors, nurses, patients**—moving about.

"Help!" Theo shouted. "I've been exposed—something's in the blood!"

A nurse rushed toward him, but then **her smile faltered**.

Theo looked around—and saw the truth. **The infection had already spread.**

Patients lay in beds, their veins pulsing black. Doctors moved from room to room with glassy eyes, whispering strange phrases under their breath. And overhead, the intercom crackled to life, repeating the same chilling message:

"It's in the blood. We are all connected."

Theo staggered backward, his mind racing. **The whole hospital was infected.** They weren't treating patients—they were **feeding the infection**, spreading it room by room.

He turned to run, but **a cold hand gripped his arm.** It was the nurse from earlier, her blackened veins pulsing under her skin.

"Don't fight it," she whispered, her voice smooth and soothing. "It's easier if you let it in."

Theo tried to pull away, but **his body felt heavy,** his limbs sluggish. The black veins under his skin spread faster, coiling around his arm, tightening like a vice.

His heart raced, pounding in his chest, but even that sound felt wrong—**as if it belonged to someone else.**

The nurse leaned closer, her breath cold against his ear. "It's not just in your blood, Theo," she whispered. **"It's in your mind."**

And that's when he felt it—**a presence**, slithering inside his thoughts, uncoiling like a serpent. It wasn't just an infection—it was **a hive**, a collective mind, feeding on fear, on pain, on life itself.

He tried to scream, but the sound **died in his throat.** His thoughts were no longer his own.

As the infection spread through him, Theo's body moved on its own—**calm, controlled**, a puppet on invisible strings. He felt himself smile, though it wasn't his smile.

He turned, calmly walking back toward the lab. The hospital around him buzzed with quiet whispers, **the hive mind awakening**.

In the distance, the intercom crackled again, repeating the message like a lullaby:

"It's in the blood. We are all connected."

And as Theo stepped into the darkened basement, the last sliver of his mind screamed, trapped beneath the infection's cold grip. **He was part of it now.**

Forever.

The Messenger

———— ◦❖◦ ————

In **Cyprus City, Italy**, nestled along the rugged coastline, **October** brought with it a strange shift—**the air grew heavier**, and the sea roared louder. Locals believed that **spirits from ancient times stirred during this season**, their voices carried by the winds that howled through the narrow streets. But the oldest, darkest tale whispered through the city was the legend of **the Messenger**—a harbinger who delivered ominous letters to those marked by fate.

No one ever saw him coming. The letter would simply appear, and once you received it, **there was no escaping what followed.**

Sofia Bernardi was a schoolteacher in Cyprus City, living a quiet life in an apartment that overlooked the sea. She loved October, with its cooler air and stormy evenings—until the morning she found **a letter resting on her doorstep**.

The envelope was **old and brittle**, sealed with a wax stamp in the shape of **an eye**, and her name was written in a shaky hand across the front. Sofia frowned—there was **no return address**, no stamp to indicate it had passed through the postal service.

She opened it slowly, and inside was a **single slip of paper** with five words:

"He comes before the dawn."

Sofia felt a chill run down her spine. **Who had left the letter?** And what did it mean?

She glanced down the street, but there was no one in sight. Just the wind, **howling through the alleys** as if it carried a warning. A heavy feeling settled in her chest, and Sofia knew—**this was no prank.**

Throughout the day, **strange things began to happen.**

A shadow flickered at the edge of her vision, disappearing whenever she turned to look. The old wall clock in her apartment **stopped at 2:13 PM**, and the air in her living room grew cold, despite the windows being shut. Her cat, **Luna,** hissed at something she couldn't see, then bolted under the couch, trembling.

By evening, **the letter seemed to pulse with a presence of its own**, resting on her kitchen table like **a curse she couldn't escape.**

She called her friend **Marco**, hoping he could calm her nerves. **"It's just a prank, Sofia,"** he insisted. **"Don't let it get to you."**

But Sofia wasn't convinced. **The letter had a weight to it—a finality.** It wasn't just a warning; it was a promise.

And as the sun set, **she heard the first knock at her door.**

The knock was soft, almost polite, but it carried **an ominous weight.** Sofia's heart pounded as she approached the door, her breath shallow and ragged. She pressed her ear against the wood, hoping to hear someone on the other side—but all she heard was **the sound of the wind, whistling through the cracks.**

She backed away, her pulse racing. **Another knock followed,** louder this time, as if whoever stood on the other side **was growing impatient.**

Sofia knew, instinctively, that **opening the door would be a mistake.**

At exactly **midnight**, the wind outside fell silent, and the knocks stopped. Sofia let out a shaky breath, thinking perhaps the visitor had gone. But as she turned toward her bedroom, **the letter on her table began to burn**—a slow, smoldering fire that didn't consume the paper but spread strange black symbols across it.

A shadow stretched along the walls, growing larger and more defined until it **formed the shape of a man**—tall and thin, his features hidden beneath a wide-brimmed hat. **The Messenger.**

He did not speak. **He only smiled,** a slow, eerie grin that stretched too far across his face.

Sofia tried to run, but **the shadows followed her**, wrapping around her like cold tendrils. She stumbled and fell to the floor, gasping for breath as the room grew darker and the Messenger stepped closer.

The Messenger knelt beside her, his presence overwhelming, like **a storm trapped inside a human form**. From the folds of his cloak, he pulled out **another letter**—this one sealed with a black wax stamp.

"For you," he whispered, placing it gently in her trembling hand. **"You are the last."**

Before Sofia could respond, **the shadows swirled around him**, and he disappeared into the darkness, leaving only the letter behind.

Sofia opened the letter with shaking hands. Inside, she found a message that chilled her to the bone:

"By dawn, one must go."

The words pulsed on the page, sinking deep into her mind. She knew what it meant—**the Messenger's gift wasn't a warning. It was a choice.** Someone in her life was marked by fate, and by the time the sun rose over Cyprus City, **either she or someone she loved would be taken.**

Tears streamed down her face as she thought of Marco—**her closest friend**, the only person who had ever truly been there for her. **Would she let him go to save herself?**

The clock struck **3:00 AM**, and she knew time was running out.

Sofia sat in the darkness, clutching the letter, her heart breaking under the weight of the choice she had to make. **She couldn't let Marco die—not for her.**

With a heavy heart, she grabbed a pen and wrote his name at the bottom of the letter. **The ink seemed to bleed through the paper**, sealing her fate.

She placed the letter on the windowsill, **offering it to the wind**, and as the first light of dawn began to break over Cyprus City, **she whispered her final goodbye.**

When Marco called her the next morning, there was no answer. He went to her apartment, only to find **the door wide open** and **Sofia's belongings left untouched.** The letter lay on the windowsill, **her name scratched out**, and at the bottom, in neat handwriting, **his name was written instead.**

Marco stared at the letter, the truth settling over him like a cold shadow. Sofia had saved him—**at the cost of her own life.**

That evening, as the sun began to set over Cyprus City, **the wind returned,** whistling through the streets with an eerie song. And somewhere, deep in the shadows, **the Messenger smiled.**

Because in Cyprus City, once you receive the letter, **the debt must always be paid**—and **the Messenger always returns.**

Sleepy Dan

In the quiet, fog-drenched streets of **Westershire**, a sleepy little borough on the outskirts of London, October was a time of strange dreams and uneasy silences. The days were crisp and gray, with damp leaves plastered to the cobblestones, while the nights were colder, cloaked in a mist so thick it seemed to **breathe**. People stayed indoors when the sun set early, not out of fear, but because that was how things were done—**you didn't wander in Westershire after dark.**

And in every whispered conversation, in pubs and schoolyards, one name surfaced again and again, as if his very mention conjured unease:

Sleepy Dan.

Sleepy Dan had become a legend in Westershire, though no one quite remembered where the story began. Children told each other that he was **a boy who never woke up**, who drifted between dreams and reality, pulling others into his nightmares. The adults dismissed it as nonsense—a silly urban myth to keep kids from causing trouble.

But every October, people in Westershire whispered about **the strange disappearances**—children and adults alike, gone without a trace, leaving behind only an unmade bed and the faintest scent of lavender. No one could explain it, but **they all knew one thing:**

Sleepy Dan always comes in October.

On the last night of the month, **Charlie Harris**, 14 years old and too brave for his own good, found himself standing in front of the **old Hargrove house** at the edge of town. His friends—Jack and Daisy—huddled close, nervously glancing at the crooked shutters and peeling paint. The house had been abandoned for years, and most people in town said it was cursed.

"This is a stupid idea, Charlie," Daisy muttered, shivering in the cold. "We shouldn't be here."

Jack nodded. "Yeah, man, let's just go back. We can say we did it."

Charlie grinned, his breath fogging the air. "Come on. You're not scared of some old house, are you?"

But the truth was, **Charlie was scared**—just a little. Not of the house, but of what lay inside. According to legend, **this was where Sleepy Dan had last been seen**—before he vanished completely, lost between dreams and waking life.

The dare was simple: **spend the night inside the Hargrove house**. But something about the way the mist curled around the windows, and how the shadows seemed to stretch, made Charlie's skin crawl.

"Just an hour," Charlie muttered, more to himself than the others. "We stay an hour, and then we go."

The door creaked open with a groan, and the three friends slipped inside, the old wood **groaning beneath their footsteps**. Dust coated every surface, and the air smelled faintly of mildew and something sweeter—**lavender**.

"Smells weird in here," Jack whispered, shining his flashlight around.

They made their way into the living room, where an **ancient armchair** sat facing a cold, empty fireplace. The wallpaper had peeled away in long strips, and the floorboards were warped and cracked.

"Let's just sit for a bit," Daisy suggested, settling nervously on the edge of the sofa. "Then we can leave."

But as they sat in silence, the house began to feel... wrong. **Too quiet.** The kind of silence that felt like it was listening.

And then they heard it—**a faint humming**, coming from upstairs.

Charlie shot Jack a look. "Did you hear that?"

Jack nodded, swallowing hard. "What... what is that?"

Daisy's voice trembled. "It sounds like... someone's humming."

Against their better judgment, the three climbed the narrow staircase, the wooden steps creaking underfoot. The humming grew louder, drifting down the hallway like a lullaby. It wasn't cheerful—it was slow and off-key, **like someone trying to remember a song from a long-forgotten dream.**

They followed the sound to a door at the end of the hall. Faded letters, scrawled in a child's hand, were still visible on the wood:

"Dan's Room."

Charlie hesitated for just a moment, then pushed the door open.

Inside, the room was frozen in time—**a child's bed**, neatly made, with a stuffed bear resting against the pillows. Dust motes floated lazily in the pale moonlight that spilled through the cracked window. On the nightstand sat an old wind-up alarm clock, its hands ticking backward.

And lying in the center of the bed, nestled beneath the covers, was a **boy**.

His skin was pale, almost translucent, and his dark hair was matted and unkempt. **His eyes were closed, but he was smiling**—a slow, sleepy smile, as if lost in the most pleasant dream.

"Is that...?" Daisy whispered, her voice barely audible.

Jack took a step back, his heart pounding in his chest. "It's him. **It's Sleepy Dan.**"

As if on cue, the boy stirred beneath the covers. His eyes fluttered open—**wide, dark, and empty**, like twin pools of midnight. And when he smiled, it was the smile of someone who knew far more than he should.

"Why are you here?" Dan whispered, his voice soft and distant, as though it came from a place far away.

The three friends froze, too terrified to answer. Dan's smile widened, but his eyes remained glassy, like those of someone who had been asleep for too long.

"You shouldn't have come," he murmured, almost kindly. "Once you step into my dream... **you can't leave.**"

Charlie's breath caught in his throat. "What do you mean?"

Dan's gaze drifted to the old alarm clock, still ticking backward. "It's not about being awake or asleep," he whispered. "It's about what follows you when you leave."

The air in the room grew thick and heavy, as if the walls themselves were closing in. The humming returned, louder this time, filling their ears until it felt like it was coming from inside their heads.

And then the boy's voice dropped to a whisper:

"Don't wake up. Whatever you do, don't wake up."

Charlie stumbled backward, dragging Jack and Daisy with him. They bolted from the room, their footsteps pounding down the stairs and out the front door. The cold night air hit them like a slap, but even outside, the humming followed—**soft and persistent, wrapping around them like a fog**.

"We have to get home," Jack panted, his voice frantic. "We have to get out of here."

But as they ran through the misty streets of Westershire, something strange began to happen—**the town seemed different.** The streets twisted and stretched in impossible ways, the houses flickering like mirages. **Streetlamps blinked in and out of existence**, casting shadows where there should have been none.

Charlie's heart raced. "This... this isn't real," he whispered, panic setting in. "We never left the house. We're still in his dream."

Daisy whimpered, clutching her head. "How do we wake up?"

The humming grew louder, and with it came a familiar voice— soft, patient, and endlessly tired.

"I told you... don't wake up."

The next morning, Westershire awoke to an eerie stillness. Charlie, Jack, and Daisy's beds were found perfectly made, **their pillows untouched**, as if they had never slept in them at all.

Their parents searched for them—called the police, knocked on every door—but there was no sign of the children. All that remained was the faintest trace of lavender in the air and the distant sound of someone humming.

And somewhere, deep within the twisting streets of a dream that had no end, three children wandered endlessly, searching for a way out that didn't exist.

To this day, in the quiet borough of Westershire, **you can still hear the humming**—if you listen closely on cold October nights. Some say it's the wind. Others say it's **Sleepy Dan**, waiting for someone else to wander into his dream.

And if you ever feel yourself drifting off on a night like that, just remember:

Don't wake up.

Because once Sleepy Dan finds you... **you'll never leave.**

The Lost Princess

The city of **Edema**, modeled after the historic streets of Edinburgh but steeped in its own eerie charm, carried an air of **mystery and melancholy** in the crisp autumn months. Every **October**, the mist rolled in from the riverbanks, cloaking the cobbled streets and whispering through the narrow alleys. And with the mist came the legend of **the Lost Princess**—a tale that haunted the dreams of those who dared stay out past nightfall.

The legend spoke of a **young princess from centuries ago**, forgotten by history, who wandered the streets of Edema in search of someone to help her find her way home. Those who encountered her said she was **beautiful and sad**, dressed in tattered silk gowns, her eyes pleading for someone to **follow her.** But no one who followed her ever returned.

It was **October 29th**, when **Clara Wells**, a university student visiting from London, arrived in Edema for the weekend. She had always loved autumn, and the city was said to be magical this time of year—its ancient stone buildings glowing under the soft yellow lights, ivy draping from windows, and pubs bustling with stories and songs.

But Clara had arrived too late—**the streets were empty**, as if the mist had swallowed the city whole. The air smelled of wet leaves and forgotten things, and as she made her way through the old town, she couldn't shake the feeling that **something was watching her.**

As she wandered deeper into the narrow streets, Clara heard **soft footsteps** behind her. She turned, expecting to see someone—a late-night wanderer like herself—but there was only **the mist,** swirling gently. And then, just ahead, she saw her.

A **young girl**, no older than twelve, stood at the edge of the fog, dressed in a **faded, once-elegant gown**, her dark hair falling over her pale face. **Her eyes met Clara's,** filled with an expression so sorrowful it stopped Clara's breath.

"Please," the girl whispered. **"Can you help me find my way home?"**

Clara's heart skipped a beat. There was something unsettling about the girl's voice—**it was too soft, too distant,** like a memory fading from a dream. But before Clara could answer, the girl turned and began walking down the alley.

"Wait," Clara called, her curiosity overpowering her fear. **"Where's your home?"**

The girl didn't answer. She **disappeared into the mist,** and without thinking, **Clara followed.**

The deeper Clara ventured into the fog, the stranger the city became. **The streets twisted,** leading her in circles, and buildings she swore she had passed earlier seemed to shift and change, as if rearranging themselves behind her back.

She called out for the girl, but **only the mist responded,** whispering her name in **soft, unfamiliar voices.**

Finally, Clara spotted the girl again—standing at the entrance of what looked like **an old garden gate**, its iron bars **rusted and twisted**, as if time had tried to erase it from existence.

The girl smiled, a sorrowful expression that sent chills down Clara's spine. **"It's just through here,"** she whispered. **"You'll help me, won't you?"**

Clara hesitated, her heart racing. **Something was wrong**—this wasn't just a lost child. **This was something ancient, something forgotten.** But before she could turn back, **the gate creaked open**, and the girl disappeared inside.

Clara knew she should leave—**every instinct told her to turn around and run.** But something about the girl's sad eyes held her in place. **She couldn't leave her alone.**

The garden beyond the gate was unlike anything Clara had ever seen. **Vines crawled across broken statues**, and flowers that hadn't bloomed in centuries lay wilted beneath the moonlight. **A stone fountain stood in the center**, filled with water so still it looked like glass.

And at the heart of the garden stood **an old stone bench**, draped in ivy. The girl sat there, her hands folded neatly in her lap, her eyes cast down.

"This was my home," she whispered. **"But no one remembers me anymore."**

Clara stepped closer, her breath visible in the cold air. **"Who are you?"** she asked, though deep down, she already knew.

The girl lifted her gaze, and in that moment, **the centuries fell away**—the air grew thick with memories of **forgotten ballrooms and empty corridors**, of songs that had once been sung in her honor. **She was the lost princess of Edema**, left behind by time, her name erased from history.

And now, she wanted Clara to stay.

The air in the garden grew colder, and the shadows deepened. **The vines around the bench began to move**, creeping toward Clara's feet, as if trying to pull her into the past.

"Stay with me," the girl whispered. **"I don't want to be alone anymore."**

Clara's heart pounded in her chest. **She could feel the weight of the centuries pressing down on her**, the sorrow of a child forgotten by the world. If she stayed, she knew she would never leave. **Her name would fade**, just as the princess's had.

But **how could she abandon her?** How could she leave the princess alone in the mist, waiting for someone who would never come?

The shadows stretched toward her, and Clara felt herself slipping—her mind growing foggy, her thoughts fading like the last notes of a forgotten song.

At the last moment, **Clara tore herself away**, her breath ragged and her hands trembling. **"I can't stay,"** she whispered, tears stinging her eyes. **"I'm sorry."**

The princess's face twisted with sorrow—**not anger, just deep, endless sadness. "They always leave,"** she whispered, her voice breaking like the petals of a dead flower. **"I'll be here... waiting."**

The garden began to crumble around her, the mist rising like a wave. **Clara ran**, her heart pounding in her chest, the whispers of the lost princess following her through the gate, through the twisting streets, until finally—**she burst into the open air.**

The mist lifted, and **the city of Edema returned to normal**, bathed in the soft light of morning. But when Clara looked back, **the alley was gone**—as if it had never existed.

Days later, as Clara prepared to leave Edema, she found **a small, withered flower** tucked into the pocket of her coat—a flower from the forgotten garden. And though the princess's voice no longer haunted her, **the sorrow lingered**, like a shadow at the edge of her mind.

Because **somewhere, deep in the mist**, the lost princess still waited—forever trapped in a garden no one remembered, waiting for someone brave enough to stay.

And **every October**, the mist would return, carrying with it **the echoes of a child forgotten by time**, hoping that one day, **someone would choose to stay.**

Captain Ulrich

The Pacific Ocean—vast, deep, and unforgiving. It is a place where **ships vanish**, and whispers of doomed voyages are carried on the winds. For **Captain Elias Ulrich**, the sea had been his home for over thirty years. He was known as **a fearless captain**, unbothered by storms or superstitions. But there are some places that even the most seasoned sailors fear—**places where the sea hides more than water and waves.**

In **October**, on what should have been a routine crossing through **the Pacific**, Captain Ulrich and his crew of twelve would discover that **some waters were never meant to be crossed.**

The journey had begun without trouble. **The Ulrich Mariner**, a cargo ship bound for New Zealand, cut through the waves with ease. But two days in, the ship's **navigation systems began to glitch.** The radar flickered, unable to maintain a steady reading, and the radio crackled with bursts of **static and ghostly whispers.**

"Just interference," Ulrich told his crew, though his gut told him otherwise. **The Pacific wasn't always kind to those who traveled it.**

By the third night, **the crew picked up a distress signal**—a faint, garbled SOS coming from somewhere deep within the ocean.

The ship's coordinates placed it near **the Devil's Triangle**, a patch of sea notorious for strange disappearances. **The signal shouldn't have existed**—there were no registered vessels in that area.

Yet the signal persisted: **"Help us... Please, help us..."**

Ulrich, against his better judgment, ordered the ship to change course. **"We're sailors, not cowards,"** he told his first mate. **"We answer distress calls."**

By midnight, **the Mariner slipped into a thick fog**, so dense that the sea itself seemed to disappear beneath them. The ship's instruments became useless—**the compass spun wildly, and GPS coordinates jumped from place to place.** The fog was like a living thing, wrapping itself around the Mariner like a shroud.

Then came **the sound**—a faint hum, rising from the depths of the ocean. It was **not mechanical**, but **organic**, like the sound of a creature **breathing beneath the water.**

As the fog parted, **the crew saw it: a massive, rusted hulk of a ship**, its name worn away by years of salt and wind. The vessel drifted silently, its decks covered in barnacles and seaweed. **No lights, no signs of life**—just a gaping emptiness that seemed to swallow the world around it.

Ulrich recognized the ship. It was **The Amara**, a cargo vessel that had **vanished without a trace** fifteen years ago. **The distress signal** they'd followed had come from a ship that wasn't supposed to exist anymore.

The crew exchanged uneasy glances, but **Captain Ulrich wouldn't back down. "We need to board it,"** he said. **"There might still be survivors."**

Ulrich and three of his men climbed aboard The Amara, flashlights cutting through the darkness. **The air was heavy and stale**, as if the ship had been adrift in the fog for an eternity. They found **no bodies, no signs of struggle**—just **abandoned equipment, half-eaten meals, and rusting tools.**

It was as if the crew had **vanished mid-step**, leaving everything behind.

And then they found **the journals**—scattered across the captain's quarters, pages torn and smeared with seawater. The final entries were scribbled frantically:

"Something came from the deep... We heard it calling... It's in the water..."

The words **chilled Ulrich to his core.**

Back aboard the Mariner, **the fog thickened**, and the temperature dropped. **The ocean turned black**, rippling with unnatural currents. The crew grew restless, whispering about **voices in the mist** and **shadows beneath the waves.**

That night, one of the sailors—**Harlan**—was found standing at the edge of the deck, staring into the water. **"It's calling me,"** he whispered, eyes wide with terror. **"It needs me."**

Before anyone could stop him, **Harlan threw himself overboard**, disappearing into the dark waters without a sound. **A ripple spread across the surface**, and from below, something stirred.

As the crew scrambled to pull Harlan from the water, **a massive shape began to rise from the depths**. It was unlike anything they had ever seen—a **serpentine mass of scales and bones**, its body coiled beneath the ship like a serpent from ancient myth.

And then it opened its **many eyes**, glowing softly beneath the waves.

The sea had claimed The Amara, and now it had come for the Mariner.

The creature **wrapped itself around the hull**, squeezing until the metal groaned and cracked. **The crew fought desperately**, but the sea had already decided their fate.

Ulrich stood on the deck, staring into the creature's endless eyes. He understood now—**this was the fate of those who entered the fog. There was no rescue, no escape.**

Only the deep.

The ship began to sink, dragged beneath the waves by **the monstrous entity** that had awakened from its slumber. **The fog swallowed the ship whole**, and one by one, the crew disappeared into the water, their screams cut short by the endless dark.

As the water closed over his head, **Ulrich heard the same whispering voice** that had drawn him into the fog:

"Welcome home, Captain..."

When the fog lifted the next morning, **the Pacific Ocean was calm,** the surface smooth as glass. There was **no sign of The Mariner** or its crew. No debris, no signal, no SOS.

Just **the vast, endless sea**—waiting for its next victim.

The End.

Project Nightshade

New Orleans in October is a place unlike any other—**where jazz lingers on the air**, and the shadows of **old stories** dance with the flickering gas lamps. It's a city steeped in history and **haunted by ghosts**, both real and imagined. But there are some things that even New Orleans keeps hidden—things not found in local legends or whispered through the streets. One of these is **Project Nightshade**, a top-secret government experiment shrouded in darkness, known only to those who **should have never spoken of it.**

This is the story of **what happens when a secret escapes—and refuses to die.**

When **Detective Leon Batiste** was assigned the case of the missing scientist, **Dr. Miranda Holt**, it seemed like a routine investigation. Dr. Holt, a biochemist, had vanished without a trace from **her lab deep within the Louisiana wetlands**, and her research had been classified almost immediately. All Leon knew was that **the government was involved**, and they weren't being honest about what Holt had been working on.

"People go missing all the time," Leon's partner had shrugged. **"Why worry about one scientist?"**

But **Leon knew New Orleans**—and he knew when something didn't add up. The last time someone disappeared under similar circumstances, **the city never recovered.**

Leon's investigation led him through **a web of lies,** but he finally found what he was looking for: **Project Nightshade,** a classified government experiment hidden beneath layers of red tape. The project was supposed to **harness the properties of a rare plant species** found only in the swamps around New Orleans—**a plant known as nightshade,** rumored to have **hallucinogenic and mind-altering properties.**

The goal? **Create a weapon**—one that could **control thoughts, manipulate fear,** and turn enemies against themselves. The government intended to use it in **warfare,** but **something went wrong** during the final trials. **Test subjects went insane,** and some of them **never came back.** Dr. Holt had been one of the lead researchers—until she disappeared.

Leon followed the trail to **an abandoned facility hidden deep in the bayou,** where Project Nightshade had conducted its final experiments. The building was **silent and empty,** except for the faint hum of power running through the walls—**as if the experiment was still active.**

Inside, Leon found **records of the project,** along with disturbing photographs: **test subjects strapped to chairs,** their faces contorted in fear. The notes described **hallucinations so real that they could kill,** induced by the plant's toxins.

And worse—**some of the subjects had escaped into the swamp.**

As Leon delved deeper into the facility, **the power flickered,** and a strange mist began to rise from the ground—**a thin, dark fog that shimmered with a faint green glow.**

Suddenly, **the walls seemed to close in,** and Leon heard whispers—**voices calling his name** in the dark. The words were soft, seductive, but filled with malice. **"Come closer, Leon... you don't belong here..."**

Leon tried to shake it off, but **the whispers grew louder,** crawling into his mind like tendrils. **The mist thickened,** swirling around him, and he realized—**the experiment wasn't over.** The nightshade plant had grown wild, **infecting the very air,** turning the swamp into **a living nightmare.**

Through the haze, **Leon saw movement—a figure limping toward him.** It was **Dr. Holt,** her eyes wide with terror, her clothes torn and soaked with swamp water.

"You shouldn't have come," she whispered, clutching his arm. **"It's not safe. They let it out—it's in the air. It's inside us."**

Leon tried to drag her out, but **the mist fought back,** wrapping around them, pulling them deeper into the shadows. **Shapes flickered at the edge of his vision**—figures made of smoke and fear, their faces contorted with rage.

"We need to go, now!" Leon hissed, but Miranda shook her head.

"There's no leaving," she whispered. **"The project doesn't let anyone leave."**

Leon realized that **the mist wasn't just an experiment—it was alive.** It fed on fear, growing stronger with every breath they took. **The voices whispered of betrayal**, of every regret and secret buried deep within his heart.

Miranda clutched his arm tighter. **"If we stop running, it will consume us,"** she said. **"But if we fight—if we stay still, it might leave us alone."**

Leon had fought plenty of battles in his life, but **nothing like this. The mist pressed in**, turning reality into fragments of horror—a vision of drowning in the swamp, his lungs filling with water, Miranda's eyes wide as she sank into the depths.

But he knew it wasn't real. **He had to fight it.**

Leon grabbed Miranda's hand, forcing his mind to focus. **"Come on,"** he whispered, pulling her through the mist. **"It's just a trick. We're getting out of here."**

They pushed through the fog, each step feeling heavier than the last. **The voices screamed in frustration**, the mist clawing at them, but Leon didn't stop. **He knew what the nightshade wanted—and he wasn't going to give it.**

Finally, they broke free—**stumbling out of the facility** and into the cold night air. **The mist swirled behind them**, hissing like a snake, but it couldn't follow. Not this time.

By the time **the government arrived**, Leon and Miranda were gone, their trail lost in the bayou. **The facility was sealed**, buried beneath layers of concrete and lies, and **Project Nightshade was officially "terminated."**

But **Leon knew the truth**—the nightshade was still out there, **waiting in the swamp**, feeding on the fear of those foolish enough to search for it.

Some nights, when **the wind howls through the streets of New Orleans**, you can still hear the whispers—**soft, seductive voices calling from the dark**.

And if you listen too closely, **you might never come back.**

The Wife's Tale

Yellowstone National Park in October is a place of breathtaking beauty—and quiet danger. **The golden aspens sway,** the scent of pine and cold air fills the lungs, and the geysers hiss like slumbering giants. But as the days shorten, **the nights grow darker**—and in that darkness, old stories stir. The kind of stories campers **ignore at their peril.**

This is the story of **one couple's final camping trip**—and **a tale that will be remembered forever in Yellowstone.**

James and Emily Greaves were experienced campers, familiar with the wilderness. They had been married for ten years, and after a rough patch in their relationship, **this trip to Yellowstone was supposed to be a new beginning**—a way to reconnect and leave their troubles behind.

They pitched their tent at **a remote campsite,** far from other campers, where **the trees stood tall** and the river whispered through the forest. **The nights were colder than they expected,** but the solitude felt perfect—just them, nature, and the chance to forget everything else.

But Yellowstone **has a way of reminding people that they are never truly alone.**

The first night passed uneventfully, the couple **sitting by the campfire**, wrapped in blankets, sipping whiskey. The moon cast silver light through the treetops, and **the forest was calm.** James told stories, **silly ones at first**, and Emily laughed like she hadn't in months.

Then, **the subject drifted**—as it always did—to **the wives' tale.**

"Ever heard about the Ranger's Wife?" James asked, poking the fire. **"Some old legend, I think."**

Emily rolled her eyes. **"Please, no ghost stories."**

But James continued anyway. **"They say a ranger's wife once disappeared in the park—left her husband without a trace. He looked for her for years, but she was gone."** He paused, eyes glinting in the firelight. **"And now, every October, campers say they see her. A woman, dressed in white, wandering through the woods, calling out for someone to come home."**

Emily shivered. **"You're ridiculous."**

"It's just a story," James said with a grin. **"What's the worst that could happen?"**

Sometime after midnight, **Emily woke to the sound of rustling leaves.** The fire had long since burned out, and the forest around them was **pitch-black**, the kind of darkness that makes you forget the world exists.

There it was again—a faint sound, like footsteps brushing through the leaves, slow and deliberate.

"James?" she whispered, nudging him awake.

He stirred, groggy. **"Probably a deer,"** he muttered, pulling the blanket over his head.

But **Emily wasn't convinced**. She listened carefully, heart pounding, as the sound **moved closer**, just beyond the glow of the dying embers.

Then came the voice—**soft, distant, and heart-wrenching**:

"James… is that you?"

Emily froze. **Her blood turned to ice.** It was a woman's voice—thin, broken, like someone who had been calling for far too long.

"James… please. Come home."

The next morning, James dismissed the incident as **a dream**, though Emily wasn't so sure. **"It felt real,"** she whispered as they packed up for a hike. **"There was a woman out there. I know it."**

James gave her a reassuring smile. **"It's Yellowstone. Sounds carry weird through the forest."**

But Emily couldn't shake the feeling that **something was watching them**, lurking just out of sight. All day, as they hiked along the river, **she felt eyes on her back**, as if the trees themselves were alive and waiting.

They returned to camp at dusk, exhausted and uneasy. James built a fire, trying to lighten the mood. But even the warmth of the flames couldn't chase away the growing sense of dread.

That night, **Emily woke again**, this time to the sound of **weeping**—soft, mournful sobs that seemed to drift through the forest like smoke.

She nudged James awake. **"Listen,"** she whispered, her heart racing.

The sobbing grew louder—**closer, as if the woman from the night before was standing just beyond the tent.**

"James… please. I need you."

James sat up, wide-eyed. **This time, he heard it too.**

"Who's out there?" he shouted, grabbing his flashlight. He unzipped the tent and shone the beam into the dark woods, **but there was nothing—only the sound of rustling leaves.**

The sobbing stopped. **And the forest fell deathly silent.**

Terrified, they decided to **leave at first light.** But when morning came, **their car wouldn't start.** The engine sputtered and died, as if **the forest itself refused to let them leave.**

Desperate, they packed their bags and began **the long hike back to the ranger station**, following the river through the dense forest. **The air was colder than before,** the sky heavy with clouds.

As they walked, **the sobbing returned**—but this time, it was everywhere, **surrounding them on all sides.**

"James, wait," Emily whispered. **"Do you see that?"**

There, standing on the far side of the river, was **a woman in white**, her hair tangled and wet, her eyes hollow and dark. **She raised her hand, beckoning to James.**

"Come home," she whispered, her voice carrying across the water. **"You promised…"**

James stared, transfixed, as if in a trance. **He began to wade into the river**, the icy water rising to his knees, then his waist.

"James, no!" Emily screamed, grabbing his arm. **"It's not real! She's not real!"**

But James shook his head, his eyes glazed and distant. **"I know her,"** he whispered. **"I have to go."**

The woman smiled—a slow, sad smile. And as she reached out to him, **her form began to twist**—her face contorting, her limbs lengthening, until she was **no longer a woman, but something far darker.**

Emily fought with all her strength, but **the current pulled James deeper** into the river, dragging him toward the waiting figure. **The water churned black**, cold as death, and James disappeared beneath the surface with **one final, gasping breath.**

Emily screamed his name, but **the forest gave no answer**—only the sound of the river rushing endlessly on.

And then, **the woman in white vanished**, leaving only **the empty river and the silence of the woods.**

Emily never found James. **The rangers searched for days,** but no trace of him was ever found—only **his wedding ring,** lying on the riverbank, as if he had left it behind.

Some say **he was taken by the ghost of the Ranger's Wife,** claimed by the forest for a promise he had forgotten. Others believe **he drowned,** his body lost to the cold currents of the Black River.

But Emily knows the truth. **Every October,** she returns to the river, hoping to see him again, to hear his voice carried on the wind.

And on the darkest nights, when the forest is silent and the moon hides behind the clouds, **she hears him calling to her** from the water:

"Emily… please. Come home."

Part III:
Creatures & Beasts

The Maker's Joke

It was the **October of 1589**, and the city of **Edenbrour**, a strange and shadowed borough of London, lay under a **shroud of mist**. The streets, normally bustling with vendors and carriages, grew eerily quiet when the autumn winds began to howl, as if the air carried whispers too dangerous to hear.

In this particular corner of the city, the people believed in **the Maker**—an unseen force, a god or trickster who toyed with fate, delivering both **miracles and horrors** at his whim. Some believed the Maker's hand guided all things; others thought him **a cosmic jester, laughing at mortal lives as they stumbled through his design**. And on rare nights, it was said, **the Maker would play his cruelest joke**—one that twisted destiny into knots, dragging the living into a fate from which they could never escape.

That **October night in 1589**, the joke began.

Bram Alistair, a clockmaker, was known throughout Edenbrour for his precision and skill. He was a man of science and reason, not prone to believing in **old tales of trickster gods or divine schemes**. His small workshop overlooked the foggy canals, and on this particular night, he worked late, crafting **an intricate pocket watch**—a gift for a nobleman's son.

As he wound the gears of the clock, a sudden **knock echoed from his workshop door.** The sound startled Bram; it was **past midnight,** and no one in their right mind would visit at such an hour. With a sigh, he set down his tools and opened the door.

Standing there was **a man draped in a long, weathered cloak,** his face obscured beneath the brim of a dark hat. **His eyes gleamed,** though no light reflected in them.

"Good evening," the stranger said with a crooked smile. **"I have something for you."**

Before Bram could respond, the man reached into his cloak and produced **a strange brass key,** etched with symbols that Bram didn't recognize.

"What is this?" Bram asked, confused.

"It's a gift from the Maker," the stranger said softly. **"His finest joke. And it's your turn to play along."**

With that, **the stranger disappeared into the mist,** leaving Bram with the key—and a growing sense of unease.

Bram turned the brass key in his hands, feeling its strange weight. He tried to dismiss the encounter as a prank—a simple oddity that meant nothing. But when he returned to his workbench, **the unfinished pocket watch lay open,** and **the key fit perfectly into the clock's winding mechanism,** as if it had been made for it.

Curious, Bram wound the key once, and the clock **began to tick**—even though he hadn't yet installed half of its gears. The hands moved smoothly, each tick resounding with a strange precision, **like a heartbeat, too steady to be natural.**

A chill ran down Bram's spine. **This shouldn't be possible.**

And yet, the watch ticked on.

Over the next few days, **strange things began to happen.** Every time Bram wound the clock, **he experienced glimpses of events that hadn't yet happened.** He saw **people's faces shift** as they aged before his eyes—he saw **conversations he hadn't yet had,** arguments that hadn't taken place. **The clock was predicting the future,** second by second.

At first, Bram marveled at his newfound power. He used the clock to **avoid accidents,** to **outwit clients,** and to **predict his rivals' mistakes.** But as the days passed, he realized something sinister: **the clock wasn't just showing the future—it was controlling it.**

No matter how hard he tried, **Bram couldn't change what he saw.** If the clock predicted a broken vase, **the vase would shatter,** even if he locked it away. If the clock showed a man dying in the streets, **Bram would stumble across the body exactly as foretold.**

The clock wasn't a gift—it was a curse. The more Bram wound it, the tighter its grip on his life became, and soon **he felt trapped in a story he couldn't rewrite.**

One night, as the fog curled through the streets of Edenbrour, Bram stared at the ticking clock on his desk, his hands trembling. **It showed an event that would happen exactly at midnight.**

A knock at his door.

A visitor stepping through.

And then, finally: **his own death.**

Panic gripped him. **He tried everything**—he smashed the clock, scattered its gears across the floor, and buried the brass key in the canal behind his workshop. But even without the clock ticking, **the seconds still passed, dragging him closer to midnight.**

At **11:59**, the air in the workshop grew cold. **The fog pressed against the windows**, and Bram could feel it—**the presence of the Maker's joke**, unfolding exactly as planned.

And then, **the knock came.**

Bram froze. **It was exactly as the clock had shown.** He thought about running—about escaping into the mist—but he knew, deep down, that **there was no escape.** The joke would play out, no matter what.

With a shaky breath, **he opened the door.**

Standing there, dressed in the same dark cloak, was **the stranger from the night he had received the key.** His smile was wider now, almost unnatural, as if **he knew the punchline to a joke Bram had yet to understand.**

"It's time," the stranger whispered. **"The Maker always takes what he's owed."**

The stranger stepped inside, and before Bram could react, **the room shifted**—the walls bent inward, the air thickened, and the light from the candles flickered and died.

Bram felt himself **falling, spiraling into darkness**, as the gears of the broken clock scattered across the floor, rearranging into a pattern he couldn't understand. **Time folded in on itself**, wrapping around him like a noose, pulling tighter with every passing second.

And as the world slipped away, Bram heard the stranger's voice one last time, **a low chuckle that echoed through the void**:

"The Maker's finest joke... is that you thought you ever had a choice."

When the townspeople arrived at Bram's workshop the next morning, **they found the door ajar**. The room was cold, and **the air smelled faintly of brass and dust**, but **Bram was nowhere to be found.**

All that remained was **the broken clock**, its hands frozen at midnight, and **the brass key** resting in the center of the floor.

The people of Edenbrour shook their heads. **Another poor soul, claimed by the Maker's joke.** And as the fog rolled back in that evening, **the story would begin again**, waiting for another fool to play along.

Because in Edenbrour, **the Maker's joke is never told just once.**

Origins

Jamestown, now a quiet coastal town, hides **a story that few remember**—a tale lost to the passing centuries. The tourists who stroll its streets in October, marveling at the historic architecture and coastal charm, don't know the **true origin of the town's name**. But **the locals know**, though they rarely speak of it.

Some say the story is **a legend**, others call it **a curse**. But the truth is far worse—a story of **betrayal, revenge, and a pact with something ancient**. And every October, the town feels **the weight of its origins**, waiting for someone to make the same mistake again.

The town wasn't always called **Jamestown**. It had no name in its earliest days, just **a settlement of desperate colonists**, trying to carve out a life on the wild shores. One of these settlers was **a man named James Walker—a surveyor by trade**, with a wife and a young son. James was well-respected, **charismatic**, and **ambitious**—perhaps too much for his own good.

In those early days, the settlers had **to rely on the land and sea**, but their crops withered, and the fish refused to bite. **Tensions grew**, and the colony's leaders **argued constantly** about how to save the town. James saw an opportunity—**if he could find a way to provide for the settlement**, he could take control of it. And that's when he made **a dangerous decision**.

One October night, James ventured alone into the **marshes on the edge of town**, following **a story told to him by an old sailor**. The man had spoken of **a creature**—an ancient spirit bound to the land, who could grant great power to those willing to **pay the price.**

James wasn't superstitious, but **desperation has a way of changing a man**. Deep in the misty marsh, he found **a small stone altar**, cracked and overgrown. And there, standing among the reeds, was **something that looked almost human—** but wasn't. Its eyes **glowed with a sickly green light**, and when it smiled, its teeth were **too sharp, too many.**

"I know what you seek," the creature hissed. **"You want the town, the power, the future. All of it can be yours... for a small price."**

James swallowed his fear. **"What do you want?"**

The creature's grin widened. **"A name."**

The deal seemed simple enough. James would offer **his own name**—in return, **the land would flourish**, and the people would prosper. **No one would know** that James had made the deal, and **no one would remember his sacrifice.**

But the creature had left out an important detail. **The land would not simply take his name.** It would take **his identity, his legacy—and eventually, his soul.**

James agreed, and **the creature vanished**, leaving behind only a whisper: **"The town is yours. But not for long."**

The next morning, **the fields were green, and the rivers were full of fish.** The people cheered James as their savior, and within days, **he was named the new leader of the settlement.** But something strange began to happen—**people forgot his name**.

At first, it was small—a neighbor would call him "sir" instead of James. Then, **his wife couldn't remember his name**, and even his own son began to look at him with confusion. Within a week, **no one remembered him at all.**

The people decided to name the settlement after **the man who had saved them**, but **no one could recall who that man was.** So they named it **Jamestown**—in honor of the nameless hero who had given them a second chance. **Only James himself remembered** the truth. He watched as **his identity slipped away**, piece by piece, until he was nothing more than **a stranger among his own people.**

As the years passed, James became **a ghost in his own life**—a shadow that no one noticed, **forgotten and discarded**, until **he faded into the land itself.**

The town thrived, but **the curse lingered**. Every October, **the spirit returns**, waiting for someone new to make **the same deal. A mayor in the 1800s, a businessman in 1923**, even **a drifter passing through in 1977**—all of them took the deal, and **all of them vanished**, leaving behind only their initials on gravestones no one remembered to visit.

The people of Jamestown have **learned to fear the marshes**— but **fear and curiosity** are two sides of the same coin. There's always someone who believes **they can beat the curse.**

In October of this year, **Elliot Graves**, an amateur historian, came to Jamestown to **uncover the truth behind its origins.** He spent hours in the town's archives, chasing **old stories** and piecing together the mystery of **the forgotten names.**

Late one evening, **Elliot ventured into the marsh**, determined to find the altar. **He found it, just as James had centuries ago—** cracked, ancient, and humming with a strange, low energy.

And there, waiting for him, was **the same creature**—its grin as sharp as ever, **its eyes glowing with that sickly green light.**

"I know what you seek," the creature whispered, just as it had done all those years ago. **"You want the truth, the story, the legacy. I can give it to you… for a small price."**

Elliot hesitated. **"What price?"**

The creature smiled. **"Just a name."**

Elliot agreed. **"I offer you my name,"** he whispered, trembling.

The creature's grin widened, and **the marsh seemed to sigh** as the deal was sealed. Elliot felt **his name slip away**, pulled from him like a thread unraveling a tapestry. ****The town would remember his work, his discoveries—**but no one would remember him.**

By the time Elliot stumbled back into town, **he was already fading from memory.** He saw his notes on display in the local museum, but **his name was nowhere to be found.** Just **a small plaque**, reading:

"Dedicated to the Unknown Historian."

Now, every October, **the story of Jamestown begins anew.** Someone always seeks **the truth or the promise of power,** and **the spirit in the marsh waits patiently**, ready to collect **another name.**

And if you visit Jamestown today, you might notice **the strange initials etched into the gravestones**, the faded markers no one remembers.

But beware—**the next time you say your name aloud**, you might find **the spirit listening**. Because in Jamestown, **names are never truly yours to keep.**

Escape the 13

In the wilds of **County Mayo, Ireland**, nestled between misty hills and dense forests, lies **Lough Morrigan**, a lake that shimmers darkly beneath the October moon. No tourists ever wander to these parts after autumn's arrival, and for good reason—**the curse of the Thirteen**. It's an ancient tale that **few believe**, but those who do refuse to speak its name aloud. The legend says that once every **October 13th**, thirteen souls are chosen—trapped within the curse of the lake, forced to face trials no mortal mind can comprehend.

The only way to survive is to **escape before dawn.**

On the cold night of **October 13th**, **Orla, Jack, Emma, and Finn**—four college friends from Dublin—set up camp near **Lough Morrigan**. They had heard rumors of the curse but dismissed them as nothing more than superstitious nonsense. The night air buzzed with laughter, whiskey-fueled stories, and the crackling of the campfire.

"So, what happens if we're cursed?" Emma asked playfully, swirling her drink.

Jack smirked. **"Thirteen people get picked, right? We're only four, so we're safe."**

The fire popped, sending sparks into the night. But **something in the air shifted**—a cold wind swept through the clearing, **snuffing out the fire instantly**, and for a moment, the forest fell silent. **Too silent.**

At **midnight**, the church bell in the distant village struck—twelve soft chimes. But then came a **thirteenth chime**, low and drawn out, reverberating through the still air like a warning.

Orla's heart pounded. **"Did anyone else hear that?"** she whispered, but no one answered. Her friends sat frozen, their faces pale, **their eyes locked on something behind her.**

Slowly, Orla turned—and saw them. **Nine figures**, dressed in ragged clothing, their faces gaunt and expressionless, standing at the edge of the forest. Their eyes burned with an unsettling, hollow light.

Thirteen souls were needed to complete the curse that night. And with Orla and her friends, **the number was now complete.**

A whisper drifted through the air, though no one spoke: **"Run."**

The thirteen figures melted into the darkness, but their presence lingered—**shadows stretching unnaturally along the ground**, ready to claim the souls marked by the curse.

Suddenly, **the friends were running**, the weight of fear pressing down on them. They stumbled through the forest, branches clawing at their clothes, the cold air biting at their skin. They had **until dawn to escape the forest**—but the curse had its own rules.

If even one of them looked back, **the shadows would take them.** If they got separated, **the forest would swallow them whole.** And worst of all—**none of them could leave until one among them was left behind.**

Escape wasn't free. It demanded sacrifice.

The forest twisted, leading them down paths that made no sense—**loops that ended in the same clearing**, no matter how far they ran. Emma tripped, her ankle twisting painfully beneath her, and the others skidded to a halt.

"Leave me!" she gasped, clutching her leg.

Jack shook his head, lifting her onto his back. **"We stay together."**

But as he said the words, **the forest seemed to laugh**, the trees creaking with unnatural joy. **The curse wanted them to believe in hope**, to think they could all make it out—but they couldn't. **One had to fall.**

And as Jack carried Emma through the twisting woods, **the shadows lengthened behind them**, waiting for their chance.

By the time they reached a clearing, **Orla felt the change in the air.** Finn had fallen behind, and the weight of **Emma's injury** was slowing them all down. **They were losing time.**

Jack panted, setting Emma down beside a tree. **"We can't keep carrying her,"** he whispered, guilt heavy in his voice.

Emma looked up, her eyes wide with fear. **"You can't leave me here."**

"There's no other way," Jack said, his voice cracking. **"If we all stay, none of us make it out."**

Orla clenched her fists, her mind racing. **Could she live with the guilt?** Was there really no other way?

But before she could make a decision, **Finn stumbled into the clearing,** gasping for breath. **"They're coming,"** he whispered hoarsely. **"They're right behind me."**

The moment Finn's words left his mouth, **the shadows surged forward,** crawling along the forest floor like a wave. **Emma screamed** as the darkness closed around her, pulling her into its cold embrace.

Her scream echoed once—and then cut off, as if swallowed whole. Emma was gone.

Jack collapsed to his knees, guilt and terror twisting his features. **"She was right there,"** he whispered, his voice breaking. **"We could have saved her."**

Orla pulled him to his feet. **"We can't save everyone. We have to keep moving."**

But the shadows weren't done. They had **claimed one soul,** but the curse was still hungry.

As they ran deeper into the woods, **the forest shifted again—** paths appearing where none had been, distant lights flickering between the trees like beacons of false hope. **The curse thrived on deception.**

At one point, Orla saw what looked like **Emma standing at the edge of the path**, her face pale but unhurt. **"Help me,"** the figure whispered, her voice distant and hollow.

Orla knew it wasn't real. But Jack stopped, staring at the figure as tears welled in his eyes. **"Emma?"** he whispered, taking a step toward her.

Orla grabbed his arm. **"It's not her. Keep moving!"**

But it was too late. **The false Emma smiled**—a cruel, twisted grin—and **the shadows pounced**. They dragged Jack into the darkness, his screams swallowed by the night.

Now, only **Orla and Finn** remained, their breaths ragged as the forest grew darker around them. The cursed figures still lurked just beyond the edge of their vision, waiting patiently for **one more soul to fall**.

They had to escape—together, or not at all.

As the first light of dawn began to break through the trees, **the final trial presented itself: a narrow bridge** over a deep ravine, with just enough room for **one person at a time.**

Finn hesitated at the edge. **"You go first,"** he said, fear in his eyes. **"I'll follow."**

Orla shook her head. **"If you stay behind, you won't make it."**

Finn met her gaze, something desperate and broken flickering behind his eyes. **"Then one of us has to run. Only one gets out."**

For a moment, **they stood in silence**, both knowing what the other was thinking. **The forest demanded a final sacrifice.**

With tears in her eyes, **Orla pushed Finn toward the bridge.** "Go!" she shouted. **"I'll hold them off!"**

Finn hesitated, but before he could argue, **the shadows surged forward, faster than ever before.**

He ran across the bridge, not daring to look back. **The moment his feet touched the other side, the shadows stopped,** retreating into the forest with a satisfied whisper. **The curse had been fulfilled.**

Finn turned, breathless, just in time to see **Orla consumed by the darkness,** her eyes locking with his one last time—**not with anger, but with acceptance.**

And then, she was gone.

Finn stumbled through the final stretch of the forest, collapsing onto the soft grass as the sun rose over the hills. **He had escaped.**

But as the morning light washed over him, he felt no relief—only the crushing weight of guilt. **The curse had been satisfied,** but at what cost?

And somewhere, deep in the shadows of **Lough Morrigan,** the thirteen souls whispered and waited. **Because the curse was never really over.**

It would return next October—**and the forest would demand more souls to play its game.**

The Bondugu's Curse

Croatia, October.

The **Mars Lands** of Croatia stretch over **a wild, haunting landscape**, where twisted trees rise from the red soil, and the air smells of decay. Locals tell travelers to **stay on the main paths** and warn them to **ignore strange smells or sounds**—especially if **they smell bread baking** deep within the forest. For that is the lure of **the Bondugu,** a cursed creature whose **hunger knows no end**.

But there is **a hidden mercy in the curse**. The Bondugu spares those who show kindness—a truth whispered from **one generation to the next**. But not everyone believes in kindness. Not everyone gets the chance.

Long ago, **Briaa** was a young boy who only wanted to help his parents. His family was poor, and **their food stores had run dry**. One day, as Briaa wandered the forest looking for **something—anything—to bring back to his parents**, he caught the scent of freshly baked bread and roasted meat.

Following the delicious smell, **he stumbled upon an old, weathered hut**, hidden beneath thorny vines. Inside was **a table piled high with food**—loaves of bread, cured meats, steaming broth, and more than Briaa had ever dreamed of seeing in his life. **His stomach growled** painfully, and he thought of his parents, weak from hunger at home.

Without thinking, **Briaa snatched a loaf of bread**, cradling it against his chest as he **ran out into the forest.**

But before Briaa could disappear into the trees, **a shadow moved at the door of the hut.** It was **an old man, hunched and pale, with sunken eyes and a wicked grin.** His gaze followed Briaa as he fled, and with a voice like rustling leaves, he whispered:

"You took what was mine, boy. Now the hunger shall follow you."

In that moment, **Briaa's body began to change.** His skin grew **leathery and gray**, his stomach twisted with an unbearable emptiness, and **his teeth stretched into jagged points.** His eyes dimmed, glowing faintly in the twilight, and **his voice turned to a low, hungry growl.**

The old man's curse was clear: **Briaa would roam the forest as the Bondugu, forever searching for food—always hungry, but never satisfied.**

Now trapped in his monstrous form, **the Bondugu wandered the Mars Lands, gnawing on anything he could find.** No matter how much he ate—**berries, roots, animals—it was never enough.** His hunger gnawed at him endlessly, driving him deeper into the forest, away from the village and the parents he had wanted to save.

Over time, the Bondugu became **a legend whispered among the villagers.** They warned travelers to avoid the forest, especially on October nights when **the scent of bread seemed to drift through the air**. But those who showed kindness were spared.

They say that if you encounter the Bondugu and **offer him food willingly, he will do you no harm.** His hunger, though endless, becomes **gentler in the presence of kindness.** Some even claim to have heard him whisper **"Thank you"** before disappearing into the night—**a small remnant of the boy he used to be.**

One cold October evening, a **young traveler named Luka** set out to camp near the edge of the Mars Lands. He had heard **the stories of the Bondugu,** but **curiosity got the better of him.** After setting up camp, Luka sat by his fire, warming a loaf of bread he had packed for the journey.

Suddenly, the **forest grew silent**. From the shadows, **two glowing eyes appeared**, and a figure stepped into the firelight—**a creature, grinning with jagged teeth, its leathery skin glistening in the dark.**

The Bondugu.

Luka's heart pounded, but instead of running, **he tore the loaf of bread in half** and held it out toward the creature. **"Here,"** he whispered. **"Take this."**

The Bondugu stopped, staring at the offering with its dim, sorrowful eyes. For a moment, it seemed **almost human,** as if the boy who once was Briaa flickered beneath the monster's exterior.

With a low growl, **the Bondugu accepted the bread,** holding it carefully in its claws. As Luka watched, **the creature's grin**

softened—just slightly—and it vanished into the shadows, leaving nothing but the faint scent of bread behind.

To this day, travelers who pass through the Mars Lands say that **the scent of bread still lingers on cold October nights**. And though the Bondugu remains a creature of endless hunger, **he does not harm those who show kindness.**

But beware—**if you cross the Bondugu's path without an offering**, he will follow you forever, until **the hunger consumes you too.**

The Locals: We Want You for Dinner

The air in **New Jersey** was unusually crisp for October. The trees lining the winding roads were cloaked in fiery reds and oranges, the scent of damp earth lingering underfoot. But beneath the festive autumn air was something rotten—**a warning carried on the wind**, one that would go unnoticed until it was far too late.

On this night, a group of college friends—**Liam, Sarah, Mason, and Jess**—were driving toward **the Pine Barrens**, eager to explore the eerie legends surrounding the infamous forest. They had heard rumors about strange sightings and people disappearing over the years. **Thrill-seekers by nature**, they thought it would be the perfect way to kick off Halloween weekend.

But as they veered off the highway onto an unfamiliar, **narrow road**, the GPS lost signal.

"I swear we should've hit the turnoff by now," Liam muttered, gripping the steering wheel.

Jess, sitting in the passenger seat, squinted at the road ahead. "This doesn't look like the Pine Barrens. Where the hell are we?"

The car headlights swept across an old, rusted sign by the roadside, **half-covered in ivy and moss**. The words, barely visible, read:

"Stenchier Township – Population 0."

Liam pulled the car over to the side of the road, frowning at the **silent, mist-shrouded town** ahead of them. "This... doesn't look right," Mason said from the backseat, shifting uneasily.

Sarah leaned forward. "We could turn back," she suggested, though her voice held more hope than certainty. "There's still time to get to the Barrens before midnight."

But curiosity had already sunk its claws into Jess. "Come on, guys! How often do we find a ghost town in the middle of nowhere? Let's check it out—it'll be fun."

Against their better judgment, **they agreed**. They got out of the car, the doors slamming with dull, hollow thuds, and wandered toward the shadowy streets of **Stenchier**.

It felt as if the town had been **waiting for them.**

The streets were narrow and overgrown, the windows of the old buildings covered with grime. **Fog clung to the ground**, swirling lazily around their ankles.

As they ventured deeper into the town, they noticed something strange: **Every house had a table set outside**. Each one was covered in dusty, rotting plates of food—steaks, loaves of bread, bowls of soup. But the food had long spoiled, the stench clinging to the air like a curse.

"This is... weird," Mason muttered, wrinkling his nose. "It's like they were about to have dinner and just... left."

Liam glanced around uneasily. **"Maybe we should head back."**

Just as the words left his mouth, they heard it—**a low, distant hum**, growing louder by the second.

And then the whisper came:

"You're just in time... we've been waiting."

The friends froze. Jess turned slowly toward the sound, her heart racing. At the end of the street, **a figure emerged from the mist**—a man with too-wide eyes and a crooked smile, dressed in clothes far too clean for a place like this.

"We're so glad you could join us," the man said, his voice dripping with mock sweetness.

"Dinner is served."

Before any of them could move, **more figures appeared**— stepping out from doorways, emerging from alleys, crawling from the shadows. **The locals** had returned, but there was something **horribly wrong** with them. Their mouths stretched too wide, revealing rows of jagged teeth, and their eyes gleamed with a hunger that was anything but human.

The air grew thick with the stench of rotting meat.

"We need to leave—now!" Liam shouted, grabbing Sarah's hand. They turned and sprinted back toward the car, the others close behind.

But the locals moved fast—**too fast**—chasing them down the streets with inhuman speed. Their laughter echoed through the night, high and shrill, like the sound of broken glass scraping against stone.

"You're ours now," they sang, their voices distorted and wrong.

"We want you... for dinner."

The group made it back to the car, hearts pounding, gasping for breath. Liam fumbled with the keys, but as he jammed them into the ignition, **the engine sputtered and died**.

"Come on, come on!" Jess screamed, slamming her fist on the dashboard.

Mason glanced over his shoulder—and his heart sank. **The locals were closing in**, surrounding the car in a perfect circle, their eyes glowing faintly in the mist.

"Lock the doors!" Liam shouted, but it was too late. **The windows cracked** under the force of pale, twisted hands slamming against them.

And then, one by one, **the doors unlocked from the outside**, as if the car itself had betrayed them.

The locals dragged them out of the car, their fingers cold and strong. **Liam, Sarah, Jess, and Mason** fought with everything they had, but the townspeople were **far stronger than they looked**.

They were carried through the streets, back to the long tables set with rotten food. **The locals hummed a strange, eerie tune** as they forced the friends into chairs, pinning them in place.

"Eat," one of the locals whispered, shoving a **moldy loaf of bread** toward Mason. His face was pale with terror, but when he tried to resist, **the hand tightened around his throat.**

"You eat," the local hissed, his eyes burning, "or **we eat you.**"

As they sat at the table, surrounded by the grinning, bloodthirsty locals, Liam realized the horrible truth. This wasn't just a ghost town—it was **a trap**.

The townspeople weren't human anymore. **They were cursed—** caught in an eternal feast, doomed to dine on those foolish enough to wander into their domain. **And now, the friends were next on the menu.**

"Let us go," Sarah begged, tears streaming down her face. "Please."

One of the locals leaned in close, his breath reeking of rot. **"Once you sit at the table,"** he whispered, **"you never leave."**

Mason snapped. In a blind panic, he reached for the moldy bread and **bit into it**, hoping it would save him. But the moment he did, **his body convulsed**—his skin turning pale, his eyes clouding over.

"No! Mason!" Jess screamed, but it was already too late.

The locals cheered, their voices rising in a twisted, joyful chorus. **"One of us! One of us!"**

Mason's head snapped toward his friends, his expression eerily calm. **He smiled.**

"Eat," he whispered. **"It's not so bad... once you get used to it."**

Liam acted on instinct, grabbing the chair leg and slamming it into the nearest local's face. **The creature shrieked**, its jaw unhinging in an unnatural way.

"Run!" Liam shouted, yanking Sarah and Jess to their feet. They tore through the streets, desperate to escape, **the locals howling behind them**.

But no matter which way they ran, **the streets twisted and shifted**, leading them back to the table, again and again.

"We can't escape," Sarah sobbed. "We're trapped!"

Liam's mind raced. **There had to be a way out.** Something the locals wanted—something that could end the curse.

And then it hit him. **A sacrifice.**

"Stay behind me," Liam whispered to Sarah and Jess. **"I'll distract them."**

Before they could argue, Liam **charged toward the locals**, throwing himself into their midst. **"Come get me!"** he shouted.

The creatures lunged, clawing and biting, but Liam kept fighting, buying time for the others to run.

"Go!" he screamed. "Get out of here!"

As Liam fell beneath the weight of the snarling locals, he heard Jess and Sarah's footsteps fade into the distance.

The last thing he saw was **the crooked smile of the leader**, leaning in close.

"Such a brave boy," the leader whispered, his breath warm and wet. **"You'll make a fine main course."**

And with that, **the feast began**.

Jess and Sarah never found their way out of Stenchier. **The streets shifted endlessly,** leading them deeper into the cursed town.

And somewhere, deep within the fog, **the locals prepared for their next meal**—their laughter rising into the night.

Because in Stenchier, **there is always room for one more at the table.**

And once you sit down... **you never leave.**

Boy Hoffer

Mozambique, October.

In the heart of **Maputo**, where dusty streets twist like labyrinths, there was a rumor among children—a whisper about **a strange house on Rua das Flores**. It looked perfectly ordinary from the outside, with **faded green shutters and a rusty gate**, but no one who entered **ever came back the same.** The children called it **"the House of No Return."**

Hoffer, an adventurous boy with more curiosity than caution, was drawn to the stories. He didn't believe in monsters or curses, and the idea of **a haunted house** was thrilling. So, one overcast October afternoon, while playing with his friends, **Hoffer decided to explore it**. His friends warned him, but **he laughed it off**, pushing open the creaking gate and stepping inside.

At first, **the house seemed perfectly normal**. The air smelled of damp wood, and dust floated in the slivers of light that leaked through cracked windows. **Old furniture sat untouched**, as if someone had left in a hurry years ago.

But as Hoffer ventured deeper into the house, **the light faded, and the air grew colder. The wallpaper peeled in strips, revealing dark, writhing stains beneath.**

And then he saw it—**a door at the end of the hall**, slightly ajar. From behind it came **faint whispers—the soft sound** of someone crying, mixed with **low, guttural murmurs**. The scent of **something vile** drifted toward him, making his stomach churn. But Hoffer's curiosity overpowered his fear. **He pushed the door open.**

What lay beyond the door was **not a room**, but **a cavernous space**, too large to fit within the walls of the house. **Pillars of bone and twisted roots** rose from the ground, and **pools of black water** reflected a sky that didn't exist. Hoffer stood frozen as **grotesque creatures** crawled through the shadows—**hulking figures with misshapen limbs**, their faces contorted into permanent sneers.

Some of the creatures were **devouring the remains of something unrecognizable**, while others **toyed with limp, unconscious victims**. The air was thick with the sound of **slurping, gnashing teeth**, and **low, eerie chants** in a language Hoffer couldn't understand.

One of the creatures looked up, its **sunken eyes locking onto him. A crooked grin spread across its decayed face.**

Hoffer stumbled back, his heart hammering in his chest. As he turned to flee, **he noticed the victims more clearly**—people **trapped in grotesque poses**, their eyes wide with terror but their bodies frozen in place, as if they were **living statues of fear**.

Some **reached out**, their mouths opening to scream—but no sound escaped. Others **wept silently**, their tears dripping into the black pools beneath them, swallowed by the dark waters.

And then Hoffer saw something that made his blood run cold: **one of the victims was a child—just like him.** A boy, frozen mid-step, with his hand stretched toward the door. His face was twisted in the same expression of terror Hoffer felt blooming in his chest.

Hoffer turned and **ran as fast as he could**, his feet pounding against the cold stone beneath him. **The creatures followed**, their laughter echoing through the cavern like the clattering of broken bones.

The door was still open, a faint rectangle of light in the distance. **He sprinted toward it**, the breath of the creatures hot on his neck. He could feel their claws **brushing against his skin**, each second stretching into an eternity.

Just as he reached the doorway, **something grabbed his ankle**, yanking him backward. He twisted, kicking frantically, and the creature hissed as it let go—**just long enough for Hoffer to scramble through the door** and slam it shut behind him.

Panting and drenched in sweat, Hoffer found himself **back in the ordinary hallway**, the sounds of the creatures fading to a distant hum. The house was quiet again, as if nothing had happened.

Without looking back, **Hoffer bolted through the front door and into the street**, gasping for air. His friends stood waiting at the gate, their faces pale with fear. **"You're lucky,"** one of them whispered. **"No one ever comes back."**

For weeks, Hoffer couldn't sleep. **He saw the creatures every time he closed his eyes.** The memory of their hungry grins haunted his dreams, and he felt **the boy's frozen stare** burn in his mind. He knew he had escaped something terrible—but **the**

house still called to him, whispering in the quiet hours of the night.

And every October, when the air turned cold and the winds howled through the streets, **Hoffer heard the same voice from behind the door**, calling his name in a low, guttural murmur:

"Come back... You left something behind..."

No one else ever saw the house again. It **disappeared**, swallowed by the shadows of the city. But Hoffer knew it was still out there—**waiting for him**, or anyone curious enough to go inside.

Unsuitable

Toronto, Canada. October wrapped the city in a crisp chill, with the golden leaves swirling across sidewalks and the scent of coffee shops mingling with the brisk air. But beneath the familiar urban charm, **something strange was brewing**. Every autumn brought a **hint of discomfort** for those attuned to it, a kind of heaviness that clung to the air. Locals brushed it off as **seasonal gloom**, but there were some who whispered otherwise.

They whispered about **unsuitable souls**—people who wandered too far, who ended up caught in things they couldn't escape. But this was **the rare exception**—one where **a mistake was made**, and **fate's hand slipped**.

This is where it all began: a **happy accident** that nearly became a tragedy.

The night of **October 12th** was supposed to be like any other. **Lila Rivera**, a 22-year-old artist from the Annex, was on her way home after an exhibit. She wrapped her scarf tighter as she walked through the quiet, tree-lined streets. Toronto's neighborhoods at night felt **safe**, familiar—until tonight.

At the edge of **Trinity Bellwoods Park**, she noticed something strange. **A group of crows gathered in silence**, perched along the fence and branches—too many to be a coincidence. As Lila passed them, they stared with **sharp, unblinking eyes**, their heads turning to follow her every step.

She shivered and hurried along. **There was something wrong about tonight.**

Lila arrived at her apartment building and slipped inside, locking the door behind her. She tossed her bag on the couch, kicked off her shoes, and checked her phone. There was a **new message from an unknown number**:

"You have been chosen. Escape the 13. You'll know when to run."

Her stomach twisted as she stared at the message. **It didn't make any sense.** She had never signed up for anything called **Escape the 13**, and it sounded more like a prank than anything serious. Yet something about the wording—**You'll know when to run**—sent a chill down her spine.

She tried to brush it off, blaming exhaustion and an overactive imagination. But deep down, **she knew this wasn't just a prank.**

Later that night, while brushing her teeth, Lila glanced out her bathroom window—and froze.

At the street corner, beneath a flickering streetlight, **twelve figures stood in a perfect circle.** Their clothes were outdated, mismatched as though they had come from **different eras**, and **their faces were turned toward her building.** Each one wore an expression of **blank indifference**, but their presence radiated a chilling menace.

Suddenly, **her phone buzzed** on the bathroom counter. Another message:

"One soul too many. You don't belong. Run."

Panic flooded her chest. The message wasn't cryptic anymore. It was **a warning.**

Without thinking, Lila grabbed her coat and phone, throwing open her apartment door. **The hallway was eerily silent**, and the elevator's hum seemed distant and wrong. She needed to get out—**now.**

As she sprinted down the stairwell, the air felt heavy, as if the walls were pressing in. **A soft hum followed her**, a low-frequency vibration that made her ears buzz and her teeth ache. She burst out into the night air, her heart hammering, and looked around frantically.

And that's when she saw them—**the twelve figures**, waiting at the end of her street, their faces illuminated by the glow of the streetlights.

But one of them was different—**a thirteenth figure**, someone who didn't belong. The figure was gaunt and crooked, its mouth stretched into a sinister grin.

And then it hit her—**they made a mistake. She wasn't supposed to be part of this. The thirteenth figure was.**

The rules were clear: **The game wouldn't start until the thirteenth soul was in place.** And that meant **Lila had one chance to escape.** She didn't belong here—this wasn't her curse to endure.

With a burst of adrenaline, she turned and ran. The streets of Toronto blurred as she sprinted through alleys and backstreets, **the wind howling at her heels**. She could hear the whispers now—low, menacing voices that curled in her ears:

"One too many... One must fall... You cannot run."

But Lila ran anyway. She ran with everything she had.

As she neared **Bloor Street**, the world around her felt distorted—the streetlights flickered erratically, and the air seemed thicker, as if she was running underwater. But just ahead, she saw it: **the bridge over the Don Valley**, glowing faintly under the moonlight. **If she could reach it, she'd be free.**

The figures chased her now, their footsteps silent but relentless. **The thirteenth figure** was at the front, its grin widening as it closed the distance between them.

Lila's lungs burned, and her legs screamed in protest, but she pushed forward, the bridge drawing closer with every step.

And just as she reached the edge—**the thirteenth figure lunged, its clawed hand outstretched.**

Lila threw herself across the bridge, her body crashing onto the pavement. **The moment her feet touched the other side**, a strange thing happened.

The figures stopped—**all thirteen of them**. They stood at the edge of the bridge, their hollow eyes locked on Lila. **The air shimmered** for a moment, and then they began to fade, as if swallowed by the night itself.

And just before the last one vanished, **the thirteenth figure grinned one final time**, mouthing the words:

"We'll see you again... soon."

Lila lay on the cold pavement, gasping for air, her heart racing in her chest. **The night was silent once more**, the streets empty and still. She had escaped—**the mistake had saved her.**

But as she picked herself up and dusted off her coat, a final message buzzed on her phone:

"You were never meant to play. Consider yourself lucky. But remember: The Thirteen always find a way."

Lila shivered, staring out into the quiet streets of Toronto. **She had escaped the game—for now.**

But somewhere, in another corner of the world, **the curse of the 13** was still waiting. And next time, **there might not be a mistake to save her.**

For now, though, **she smiled**—because this was her story's **happy ending.**

The Will

⋯•✦•⋯

It was the first week of **October**, and the winds in the small New England town of Ashford carried the scent of rotting leaves and distant rain. The residents were preparing for Halloween, but for the **McAllister family**, a different kind of gathering was underway.

They were gathered in the **study** of the family's crumbling ancestral estate, summoned by the death of **Douglas McAllister**, the family patriarch. The house, much like its owner, was old and tired—a shadow of its former glory, filled with dark hallways, peeling wallpaper, and the ghosts of **forgotten wealth**.

The only thing left that mattered was **the will**.

Douglas had been a strange and secretive man, growing more paranoid and bitter with each passing year. None of his three children—**Victor, Claire,** and **Andrew**—knew exactly what to expect from his inheritance. They only knew one thing: **the will would determine everything.**

The family lawyer, **Elliot Banks**, arrived just before dusk. A thin, pale man with nervous eyes, Banks clutched the old leather briefcase containing the will as if it were a bomb waiting to explode.

"You should know," Banks began hesitantly, as the siblings sat in the cold, dimly lit study, "your father... made some unusual arrangements in the final draft of his will."

Victor, the eldest and most impatient, scoffed. "Of course he did. The old man was always playing games."

Claire shot him a warning glance but said nothing, wringing her hands in her lap. Andrew sat quietly in the corner, his face pale and drawn, as though the house itself weighed on his spirit.

Banks cleared his throat. "Your father insisted that the will must be **read in full tonight**, under no circumstances to be delayed. He was... quite insistent."

Victor rolled his eyes. "Get on with it, then."

Banks nodded, pulled out the yellowed sheets of paper, and began to read.

"To my children," Banks read, "I leave my estate and all its contents—but only under the following conditions."

Victor leaned forward, smirking. "Here we go."

Banks continued, his voice trembling slightly. "The house and everything within it will belong to the last of you **to survive the night**."

The room fell into stunned silence. Claire's breath hitched. Andrew shifted uncomfortably in his chair, his eyes darting to the darkened corners of the room.

"What the hell does that mean?" Victor demanded, his voice sharp with disbelief.

"There's more," Banks whispered. "He... left instructions."

Banks read on: "The doors and windows will be sealed as soon as this will is read. None of you will be able to leave until **dawn**. The one who remains in the house by first light will inherit everything. If more than one of you remains... the house will choose."

"The **house** will choose?" Claire whispered, her voice barely audible.

At that moment, a deep **groaning noise** echoed through the house, like ancient wood settling. The sound reverberated through the walls, making the floor beneath their feet tremble.

Then, with a loud **thud**, the windows and doors **slammed shut**, trapping them inside.

Victor shot to his feet, yanking at the door handle. It didn't budge. "What the hell is this?!" he shouted, slamming his fists against the wood. "This is insane!"

Claire stood as well, glancing nervously at Andrew. "It's just a trick," she said, though her voice trembled. "Right?"

Andrew said nothing, his wide eyes fixed on the dark hallway beyond the study door.

Banks, pale as a ghost, gathered his papers and stood. "The terms are binding. You must remain in the house until dawn."

Victor glared at him. "And what happens if we don't?"

Banks hesitated, swallowing hard. "He... said the **house would deal with you.**"

Victor cursed under his breath and grabbed the fire poker from the hearth. "Well, we're not just sitting here waiting for some imaginary curse to play out."

But before anyone could react, the lights flickered—**once, twice, then went out completely.**

The room plunged into darkness, save for the weak glow of the fireplace. The shadows seemed to **stretch and twist**, creeping along the walls as if they had lives of their own.

And then came the **first whisper**.

It drifted through the room, faint and unintelligible, like a voice speaking from the other side of a veil. Claire clutched her brother's arm. "Did you hear that?"

Andrew nodded, his face pale. "It... it sounded like him."

"It's not him," Victor snapped, gripping the fire poker tighter. "It's just the house. It's trying to scare us."

The whisper grew louder, more distinct, and now they could hear **words**—words spoken in their father's voice.

"You shouldn't have come back," the voice whispered. "You all left me... but I never left."

Victor backed away from the shadows, shaking his head. "It's a trick," he muttered. "It has to be."

But then the voice changed—warped and distorted, becoming something **not entirely human.**

"One of you will stay. One of you will join me."

Without warning, the study door **slammed open**, and the cold air from the hallway rushed in, extinguishing the fire in the hearth. The room plunged into absolute darkness, and for a moment, all that could be heard was the frantic breathing of the siblings.

Then came the **scream**.

It was Claire. She was yanked backward into the hallway, disappearing into the shadows. Her screams echoed through the house, growing more distant, until they were silenced with a **sickening snap**.

"Claire!" Andrew cried, lunging toward the open door, but Victor grabbed him, pulling him back.

"No!" Victor hissed. "She's gone! If you follow her, you'll be next."

Andrew stared at him in disbelief. "We can't just leave her!"

Victor shook his head, his face pale. "We don't have a choice."

The whispers returned, louder and more insistent, swirling around them like a storm. The house groaned again, as if shifting on its foundations, and the air grew thick with **something ancient and hungry**.

Victor gritted his teeth. "We just need to make it until dawn," he whispered. "If we stay together, we can—"

The sentence died on his lips as the shadows began to **move**, creeping along the walls toward them. The floorboards beneath their feet **shifted**, and the walls seemed to pulse, breathing like a living thing.

"Run," Andrew whispered, grabbing Victor's arm. "We have to run."

The brothers sprinted through the house, their footsteps echoing through the empty halls. But no matter which way they turned, the house twisted and turned with them, **the walls closing in**, forcing them deeper into its heart.

They stumbled into an old bedroom, slamming the door behind them. The walls were covered in peeling wallpaper, and a **cracked mirror** hung crookedly on the far wall.

Victor sank to the floor, gasping for breath. "We just need to wait it out," he whispered. "A few more hours. We can make it."

Andrew stared at the mirror, his reflection flickering like a faulty image on an old television screen. "Victor..." he whispered. "Look."

Victor turned toward the mirror—and saw **himself**, standing just behind Andrew, holding the fire poker in his hand.

Except... **Victor hadn't moved.**

The reflection smiled—a wicked, distorted grin. **"The house has chosen."**

Before Victor could react, Andrew's body **collapsed**, lifeless, his eyes wide with terror.

The fire poker fell from Victor's hand as the whispers closed in, wrapping around him like chains.

When the first rays of sunlight pierced the windows, the house fell silent. The doors unlocked. The shadows retreated into the walls, and the groaning ceased.

The lawyer, Elliot Banks, returned just after sunrise, as instructed.

He found the house empty, save for **one figure** standing in the study—Victor, his eyes vacant, his face pale as death.

"The house has chosen," Victor whispered.

And then, with a slow, eerie smile, he **turned to the lawyer.**

"Your turn."

Part IV:
Distorted Realities

The Hangers

New Zealand's wilderness is known for its breathtaking beauty—**lush green forests, towering mountains, and quiet, mist-covered valleys**. But hidden deep within the remote areas of the Southern Alps lies a place few dare visit. It's known as **The Hangers**—a stretch of rugged cliffs and gorges where things have a habit of... **sticking around**.

The name came from the way **objects—and sometimes people—would be found suspended**, tangled in trees or caught on the jagged cliffs. Locals called it **an accident waiting to happen**, but every October, the stories resurfaced—stories about hikers who went missing, only for their **belongings to reappear, hanging in strange places**, untouched by time. Some claimed the area was haunted, others whispered of a curse.

This year, however, **the truth would reveal itself**—in ways no one could ever imagine.

It was **October 20th**, and a group of three friends—**Leo, Natalie, and James**—set out on a weekend hike to The Hangers. They'd heard the stories, of course, but they were experienced hikers, **skeptics**, and eager for a new adventure. Natalie joked, **"If we get stuck up there, at least we'll be part of the legend."** They all laughed—nervous, but excited.

The sky was overcast as they began their climb, **the forest strangely silent** except for the occasional rustling of leaves in the wind. The air smelled faintly of damp earth and old moss, and the trail wound upward into the mist-shrouded cliffs.

Hours passed without incident, but as they reached the narrow ridges of The Hangers, the wind picked up, howling through the gorges. **That's when things started going wrong.**

Leo was the first to notice something strange. **His jacket was gone**—vanished from his backpack, though he swore he had packed it. They laughed it off at first, assuming he'd dropped it somewhere along the trail. But soon, **Natalie's water bottle disappeared**, and then **James' flashlight**, as if the forest was slowly **picking them apart**.

"It's the stories, right?" James muttered nervously. "The Hangers... where things just disappear."

But this wasn't just coincidence. **The forest was taking things—** and it wasn't done yet.

As night fell, the friends reached a narrow clearing near the cliff's edge. **The fog rolled in thick**, and their lanterns cast only faint, flickering light. They decided to set up camp for the night, hoping the weather would clear by morning.

That's when **they saw it**—something moving in the fog.

At first, it looked like **branches swaying** in the wind. But as the mist thinned for just a moment, they saw it clearly: **figures hanging from the trees**, tangled in branches, swaying unnaturally in the wind. **Clothes, backpacks, even old shoes—**

all suspended, as if something had taken them and left them to dangle in the forest like forgotten ornaments.

And then **one of the figures moved.**

It wasn't just objects that were hanging—it was people. **A hiker, still alive but twisted and frozen**, his limbs tangled awkwardly in the branches. His eyes were wide with terror, his mouth open in a silent scream, as if he'd been trapped for **years.**

Natalie screamed. **"We need to go. Now."**

As they scrambled to leave, **the forest came alive**. The trees groaned, shifting as if stirred by a terrible, ancient force. **The ground beneath their feet felt unstable**, and shadows slithered through the mist, circling them like hungry predators.

Then **James was lifted off the ground.** One moment he was running beside them, and the next, he was yanked upward—**his body twisting violently**, tangled in an invisible force. **He dangled helplessly**, his limbs jerking like a puppet, eyes wide with disbelief.

"James!" Leo shouted, but there was no way to reach him. The forest had taken him—**claimed him as part of its collection**.

Leo and Natalie ran blindly through the forest, the **fog swallowing their footsteps**. The wind howled around them, carrying the faint sound of **James' panicked breaths**, which grew fainter and fainter. Every now and then, they would see objects **floating through the mist**—jackets, hats, water bottles—**things left behind by those who had come before them.**

The forest **wanted them, too**. It wanted them to stay.

They finally reached the edge of the cliff, where the narrow trail led back down to safety. But as they scrambled over rocks and roots, **Natalie tripped**—and before Leo could reach her, she was **lifted into the air**, her body twisted by the same invisible force.

She looked at Leo, eyes wide with terror, as her body was slowly pulled into the trees, her voice a faint whisper: **"Run."**

And then she was gone, **swallowed by the mist**, dangling among the forest's many victims.

Leo made it back to town at dawn, **his face pale and his eyes empty**, haunted by what he had seen. No one believed his story—no one ever believed the stories about The Hangers. They told him he must have gotten lost in the fog, hallucinated from exhaustion. They sent search teams, but they found nothing—**no sign of James or Natalie**.

But Leo knew the truth.

The forest doesn't take everyone. It only takes **some**, leaving the rest to tell the tale—to keep the story alive.

And every October, the wind whispers through the cliffs, carrying with it the sound of **laughter, panicked breaths, and distant screams**—reminders of the souls still trapped, hanging just out of reach.

And if you ever wander too far into The Hangers, **you might find them still swaying in the trees**—a shoe, a jacket, a backpack... and sometimes, **a person**, caught forever in the forest's grip.

And you'll know then, as the mist closes in, that you're next.

The Locals

In **Stenchier**, a sleepy, fog-choked village nestled along the rugged cliffs of the English coast, nothing much ever happened. The sea rolled in and out, fishermen hauled their daily catch, and the residents kept to themselves. Visitors rarely stopped by, and the locals preferred it that way. Life was quiet, predictable.

But this **October**, everything changed. Something stirred in the air—something that made the townspeople restless and strange. It began with **whispers on the wind**, carried in from the sea, and ended in **bloodshed**.

And by the time anyone realized what was happening, it was **too late to leave**.

Tom Mercer, a freelance journalist, arrived in Stenchier on a foggy morning in mid-October. He had come to investigate the strange stories trickling out of the village—**violent outbursts, missing people**, and an eerie silence from the residents who remained.

Tom expected to find nothing more than **superstition and gossip**, but as soon as he set foot on the cracked cobblestone streets, he knew something was wrong. The village was too quiet. No children played outside, no fishermen called from the docks. The only sound was the distant roar of the sea and the occasional **bang of a shutter slamming against a window** in the cold wind.

As Tom made his way to the inn, he noticed the **stares**. Locals stood in doorways and windows, their faces half-hidden in the fog, watching him with **cold, empty eyes**.

He gave them a polite nod. **No one smiled back.**

The innkeeper, a wiry old woman named **Mrs. Hollow**, gave Tom a room at the back of the building. She barely said a word, only handing him the key with a shaking hand.

"You'll leave before sundown," she muttered, avoiding his gaze.

Tom raised an eyebrow. "I was hoping to stay for a couple of days. I'm writing an article about the village."

Mrs. Hollow's face tightened. **"No one stays here after dark,"** she whispered. "Not anymore."

When Tom asked why, **her only answer was the sound of the door slamming behind her.**

Determined to find out what was going on, Tom spent the day wandering the narrow streets. The village looked normal enough—quaint stone cottages, fishing boats tied up at the docks, a small church with a crooked steeple. But the longer he walked, the more he noticed the signs that something was off.

Windows were boarded up, **as if expecting a storm**, though the forecast predicted clear skies. Doors were chained shut from the outside. And everywhere he went, the locals followed him with **silent, accusing eyes**.

It wasn't just curiosity—they were watching him, like **a pack of wolves tracking prey**.

When he stopped to ask a woman about the strange atmosphere in the village, she only muttered, "You shouldn't have come."

"Why not?" Tom asked, but she **hurried away without answering.**

As the sun began to dip toward the horizon, Tom made his way back to the inn. Mrs. Hollow was waiting at the door, her face pale with fear.

"Leave, now," she hissed, glancing nervously at the street. "You don't know what happens here after dark."

Tom frowned. "What happens?"

She hesitated, her eyes darting toward the shadows gathering along the road. Then, in a trembling voice, she whispered:

"They change."

Before he could ask what she meant, she slammed the door in his face, bolting it from the inside.

Tom turned around, a knot forming in his stomach. **The streets were empty now**, and the wind carried a strange sound—a low, eerie **hum** that seemed to come from the very ground beneath his feet.

And then he saw them.

The locals, standing motionless at the far end of the street, their eyes gleaming in the twilight. They no longer looked human.

Their mouths twitched into twisted smiles, **teeth too sharp** and **skin too pale**, and their eyes—once dull—now burned with **a terrible hunger.**

Tom backed away, his heart pounding. He tried to run, but the locals moved **too fast**, sprinting toward him with an inhuman speed.

He ducked into a narrow alley, his breath ragged, and watched as they swarmed the streets like a pack of wild animals, **howling and snarling**. He could see more of them now—**men, women, children**, all transformed into something **feral** and **bloodthirsty**.

The wind picked up, carrying a chorus of laughter—**high, shrill, and wrong**. It wasn't just a game. **They were hunting him.**

Tom pressed himself against the cold stone wall, hoping the shadows would hide him. He held his breath as the first of the locals passed, sniffing the air like a predator tracking prey.

For a moment, he thought he was safe.

Then a voice, soft and playful, whispered from the darkness:

"We can smell you."

Tom bolted, his legs burning as he sprinted through the winding streets. The locals followed, their footsteps echoing through the night like a drumbeat.

"Come play with us!" one of them shrieked, her voice distorted and jagged, as though her throat were filled with broken glass.

He stumbled through the village square, knocking over barrels and crates in a desperate attempt to slow them down. But no matter how fast he ran, **they were always just behind him**—laughing, snarling, their eyes glowing like embers in the dark.

At the edge of the village, Tom spotted the small, crooked church. The doors were **ajar**, and a faint light flickered inside.

With no other option, he ran toward it, throwing himself through the door and slamming it shut behind him. The locals gathered outside, their distorted faces pressed against the windows, **grinning and snarling** like animals.

Tom backed away from the door, his heart pounding. The church was dimly lit by a few flickering candles, and the air smelled of damp wood and old wax.

And then he saw it—**something scrawled on the walls**, written in a strange, jagged script. **A warning, left by those who came before him.**

"The curse spreads with the wind. Once you breathe it in, there's no going back. They are the first. We will be next."

Beneath the message was **a symbol**—a spiral, drawn in red, with lines radiating outward like the spokes of a wheel.

Tom's breath hitched. **The curse wasn't just in the people.** It was in the very air, carried on the wind. And once it found you, **it never let go.**

The door shook violently as the locals slammed against it, their laughter echoing through the small church.

Tom backed toward the altar, his hands trembling. He knew he couldn't fight them—not all of them. But maybe, just maybe, he could **survive until dawn.**

He grabbed a heavy wooden cross from the altar, gripping it like a weapon. The laughter outside grew louder, more frenzied, as the door began to splinter.

And then, in the flickering candlelight, **he saw something move**—a shadow stretching across the walls, crawling closer with every passing second.

It wasn't the locals.

It was something **worse.**

The locals weren't just cursed. **They were vessels**—empty shells, filled with something ancient and hungry, waiting to break free.

And now, it was coming for Tom.

The candles flickered out, one by one, as the door burst open. **The locals flooded in**, their faces twisted with delight.

Tom raised the cross, but it was no use. The shadows swallowed him whole, dragging him into the darkness.

And as the church filled with shrill, inhuman laughter, the wind outside carried a new sound—a whisper, soft and cruel:

"Welcome to Stenchier."

When the sun rose over Stenchier, the village was silent once more. The streets were empty, the windows shut tight. There was no sign of Tom Mercer or the others who had come before him.

But the air still carried a faint, lingering hum—a sound that drifted out to sea, waiting for the next traveler to arrive.

And the locals? They went back to their lives, waiting patiently for the **next October**, when the wind would carry the curse once more.

Because in Stenchier, **nothing ever leaves.**

The Gallows

In the heart of **Castello del Fiore**, an ancient Italian village hidden deep in the Tuscan hills, there is a place the locals fear above all: **the Gallows Hill**. The old stone gallows stands crooked and weathered, overgrown with ivy, a relic from a time when the condemned met their end beneath its hanging noose. No one has used it in centuries, but the stories linger—whispers of **vengeful spirits** and **unholy curses** that wake every **October**, when the winds shift and the shadows stretch longer than they should.

They say that once a soul swings from the gallows, **it never leaves.**

It was **October 28th** when **Luca Ferrante**, along with his friends, **Dario** and **Camilla**, made the reckless decision to visit Gallows Hill. They were young, bored, and eager to do something daring before the annual **Autumn Festival**. The warnings from their parents—stories of lost travelers and strange voices heard near the gallows—only made the place more tempting.

"It's just an old legend," Luca said with a grin, leading the way up the winding path that snaked through the hills. "We go up, take a few pictures, and come back heroes. Easy."

Camilla shivered, pulling her jacket tighter around her. **"What if the stories are true?"**

Dario rolled his eyes. "The only thing we'll find up there is a bunch of old stones."

As they climbed higher, the wind howled through the trees, carrying with it the faint scent of **decay and damp earth**.

But none of them noticed how **the birds had gone silent**.

The trio reached **the summit** just as the last light of day faded. The gallows stood before them—**a twisted, ancient structure**, its wooden beams bleached pale by time and weather. The noose, frayed and tattered, still hung from the crossbeam, **swaying gently in the wind**, though there was no breeze strong enough to move it.

"Creepy," Camilla whispered, her breath visible in the cold night air.

Luca, emboldened by their journey, stepped toward the gallows. "It's just wood and rope," he said, grabbing the noose. **The rope felt strangely warm**, as if someone had only recently used it. He laughed nervously, but there was an edge to his voice.

Dario pulled out his phone. "Alright, let's get a picture and get out of here."

But just as the camera clicked, **the wind shifted**—cold and sudden, blowing leaves and dust into the air.

And then, without warning, **the noose tightened in Luca's hand.**

Luca dropped the rope, stumbling back in shock. "What the hell..." he muttered, shaking his hand. A red welt had appeared around his wrist, **as if the rope had burned him.**

Camilla's eyes widened. "We should leave," she whispered.

But **it was already too late.**

The air around them grew heavy, the shadows deepening until the world seemed bathed in a sickly twilight. **The noose swung wildly** on its own, twisting and coiling like a snake. And then... they heard it.

A creak.

The sound of a wooden beam straining beneath weight—**as if someone had stepped onto the gallows.**

Luca, Dario, and Camilla stood frozen, their hearts pounding in their chests.

"Do you hear that?" Dario whispered, his voice barely audible.

Before anyone could answer, **a shadow appeared on the gallows**—a tall, emaciated figure, wrapped in tattered robes, **its head tilted at an unnatural angle**, the noose tight around its neck.

The figure **twitched**, its lifeless eyes fixed on the three friends. And then it spoke, its voice a raspy whisper, carried on the wind:

"One of you must swing."

Panic surged through the group. "This isn't happening," Luca whispered, backing away. **"This isn't real."**

The figure on the gallows twisted its neck toward him, the sound of bones cracking filling the air. **"One of you,"** it repeated, its voice devoid of emotion. **"Or all of you."**

Dario grabbed Camilla's hand. "We need to run. Now."

But as they turned to flee, **the path behind them vanished—** swallowed by the encroaching shadows. The only way out was through the gallows.

"We're trapped," Camilla whispered, tears brimming in her eyes.

Luca stared at the figure, his heart hammering in his chest. "It wants a sacrifice," he said, his voice hollow. **"One of us... or it won't let us leave."**

Dario shook his head, panic written across his face. "No way. We're not doing this."

The figure's head twitched again, its noose tightening with an eerie creak. **"Choose, or the choice will be made for you."**

Camilla sobbed, clutching Dario's arm. "We can't—"

But Luca knew. **It was him or them.**

His mind raced, the weight of the decision suffocating. **If he didn't act, none of them would leave alive.**

"I'll do it," Luca whispered, stepping toward the gallows.

Dario grabbed his arm. "Luca, no!"

But Luca shook him off, his face pale and resolute. **"I have to."**

Luca climbed the wooden steps, his breath coming in shallow gasps. **The noose seemed to reach for him**, curling around his neck like a lover's embrace. He could feel **the cold fingers of the past** wrapping around his soul, pulling him into the endless void of the condemned.

As he stood on the platform, **the figure grinned**—a smile too wide, filled with rotting teeth.

"Thank you," it whispered, its voice a mixture of relief and malice. **"You are one of us now."**

The trapdoor beneath Luca's feet swung open, and for a brief moment, he felt the sickening lurch of freefall. **The noose snapped tight.**

Camilla screamed, covering her mouth in horror as Luca's body swung gently from the beam.

For a moment, the air was still. The figure on the gallows faded into the night, **its place taken by Luca's lifeless body**, swaying gently in the wind.

But as Dario and Camilla turned to leave, thinking the nightmare was over, **they heard the creak again**—the sound of another beam bearing weight.

They looked back in terror. **Luca's body was no longer hanging alone.**

Two new nooses swayed beside him—**waiting**.

And slowly, as if drawn by an invisible force, **Dario and Camilla began to move toward the gallows**, their feet dragging against the ground, their minds no longer their own.

Years later, travelers passing through Castello del Fiore would occasionally spot **three figures swinging gently from the ancient gallows**, their faces pale and twisted in eternal agony.

The locals never spoke of it. **They knew better.**

Because the legend was clear—**the gallows always takes what it's owed.** And once it has a taste for souls, it never stops.

Every October, the nooses swing in the cold wind, **waiting for the next foolish travelers** to wander too close.

And as the wind howls through the trees, the gallows whispers its eternal warning:

"One of you must swing..."

Bonus: Locker 42

O ctober in Seoul brought a damp chill that settled in the air, making the hallways of **Haesong University** feel darker than usual. The **campus lockers**, tucked away in the old building, were infamous among students, but none was more notorious than **Locker 42**. For years, it was said that **the ghost of a girl** haunted the locker, her **head sealed inside**, waiting for someone to open it and set her free.

No one knew who she was, but everyone knew the story—**a tale of betrayal, jealousy, and tragedy**, passed down from one class to the next. It was the kind of urban legend people whispered to scare each other, but no one took seriously.

Until this October, when **the whispers became real.**

On the night of **October 30th**, a group of students—**Jisoo, Minho, and Hana**—gathered in the old building. It was the perfect setting for a dare, with **its flickering lights and cracked walls**, the kind of place where urban legends thrive.

Jisoo grinned as she pointed toward **Locker 42**. **"I dare you to open it,"** she whispered to Minho, her eyes gleaming with mischief.

Minho scoffed. **"It's just a story,"** he said, trying to sound brave. But the truth was, **something about the locker unsettled him.**

The dull metal door looked harmless, but it carried the weight of **decades of fear**—fear that was almost tangible.

Hana nudged him. **"Come on. Are you really scared of a locker?"** she teased.

Minho rolled his eyes and stepped forward. **The lock had long been broken**, and as his hand hovered over the handle, the air around them grew heavy—**as if the building was holding its breath.**

With a deep breath, Minho yanked open the locker door.

At first, there was nothing inside—just **dust and a faint, musty smell**. He exhaled, laughing nervously. **"See? Nothing."**

But then Hana screamed.

Minho turned, and there it was—**a severed head**, resting at the bottom of the locker. **Its eyes were wide open**, staring blankly into the void, and its long, black hair spilled out across the floor like a river of shadows. The mouth hung slightly open, frozen in an expression of silent terror.

"That's impossible," Minho whispered, backing away. **"It can't be real..."**

And then **the head blinked.**

The locker door slammed shut on its own, and **the lights flickered violently**, plunging the hallway into near darkness. The temperature plummeted, and a whisper drifted through the air, soft and chilling:

"Find my body... or take my place."

Jisoo gasped, her breath visible in the freezing air. **"What does that mean?"** she whispered, but Minho already knew—they had disturbed something that **should have remained sealed.**

The ghost wasn't just trapped. She was waiting.

They tried to run, but **the hallway twisted** into an endless loop, leading them back to **Locker 42** no matter which direction they took. **The ghost's whisper grew louder,** curling around them like a noose.

"Find my body... or take my place."

Hana began to cry. **"What does she want from us?"**

Jisoo shook her head, her voice trembling. **"We have to find the rest of her. If we don't, one of us... one of us will become her."**

With no other choice, the group began searching the old building, looking for **any clue about the ghost's body.** They checked **storage rooms, basements, and old classrooms,** but found nothing—until they reached the **abandoned gymnasium.**

There, hidden beneath a pile of decaying mats, was **a tattered school uniform**—and beneath it, **a crumpled skeleton.**

Hana let out a choked sob. **"This must be her..."**

But as they reached for the remains, **the lights in the gym flickered,** and the ghost's voice echoed through the room:

"Too late."

The air turned icy as **the ghost materialized before them,** her **severed head hovering** just above the body. **Her hollow eyes**

locked onto Minho, a twisted smile spreading across her pale face.

"Take my place," she whispered, her voice a sickening mix of sorrow and delight. **"Or you'll all stay here... forever."**

Minho knew there was no other way. **Someone had to stay.** The ghost demanded it.

With a heavy heart, he looked at Jisoo and Hana. **"Go. Get out of here."**

"No!" Hana cried, grabbing his arm. **"We can't leave you!"**

But the hallway around them began to close in, **the walls shifting and groaning** as the curse tightened its grip. **Minho gave them one last, sad smile.**

"It's the only way."

As Jisoo and Hana sprinted down the hall, **the ghost turned toward Minho,** her cold hands reaching out. **The locker creaked open,** waiting for its new occupant.

"I'm sorry," Minho whispered, his voice barely audible over the ghost's whispers. **"I didn't mean to..."**

The last thing he saw was the inside of **Locker 42,** cold and dark, as **the door slammed shut behind him.**

When Jisoo and Hana told the school staff what had happened, **no one believed them.** The old building was searched, but there was **no trace of Minho**—only an empty locker with his name scratched into the metal.

The teachers dismissed the story as **a prank gone wrong**, but **the students knew better**. They whispered the truth to each other in hushed voices:

Locker 42 wasn't empty anymore.

It had a new occupant—and once October rolled around again, **it would need another.**

Bonus: The Tattered Girl and the Ruben

Japan in October holds a kind of quiet magic—**the red maples lining ancient paths, the cool breeze whispering through shrines, and a sense of change lurking in the air.** But not all change is welcome. Some things that linger in the autumn winds are better left unseen. In the sleepy mountain village of **Komorimura**, there is a story whispered among locals, a warning spoken only in the fading light of dusk—**"Beware of the Tattered Girl."**

It's said that **she waits** at the edge of the forest, wearing **a dress of frayed ribbons,** her face hidden beneath dark hair. If you ever **meet her eyes,** you'll be marked. And once marked, **the Ruben**—a cursed spirit—will come for you.

Haruto and Aiko, two university students from Tokyo, had come to **Komorimura** for a weekend of photography and folklore. Haruto had always been obsessed with legends, and he wanted to capture the eerie beauty of the **mountain forests** before winter arrived.

"We should find the forest where the Tattered Girl was seen," Haruto said eagerly, his camera dangling from his neck. **"Imagine the photos we could get."**

Aiko wasn't convinced. **"It's just a story, Haruto. We shouldn't push our luck."**

But the more she protested, the more Haruto's curiosity grew. **By late afternoon,** they were walking the narrow path into **the forest**, mist rising from the ground as the shadows grew longer.

They had barely stepped into the forest when **Aiko spotted something strange—a flicker of movement** among the trees, just at the edge of her vision. **A girl**, she thought, standing still, dressed in what looked like **tattered strips of cloth**, barely visible beneath the canopy's dappled light.

"Did you see that?" Aiko whispered, her voice trembling.

Haruto glanced around but saw nothing. **"See what?"** he asked, raising his camera.

"A girl... over there. She looked—" But before Aiko could finish, **the figure was gone**, swallowed by the mist.

They continued deeper into the forest, and the sense of **unease grew heavier**. The air grew colder, and the forest grew eerily quiet—no birds, no wind, just the sound of **their footsteps crunching on dead leaves.**

Suddenly, Aiko gasped, clutching her hand. **"Something touched me,"** she whispered, her eyes wide with fear. **"It felt cold."**

Haruto checked her hand, but there was **nothing visible**—no mark, no scratch. But Aiko knew. **She could feel it.**

Something had **brushed against her soul**, and now it was **following her.**

By the time they reached **the clearing**, the sun had dipped behind the mountains, leaving only a faint glow on the horizon. **The fog thickened**, swirling at their feet, and with it came **a strange hum**—a sound like distant chanting, growing louder with every step.

Haruto's heart raced as he scanned the trees with his camera, but the lens only revealed **shadowed shapes**, twisting and writhing among the branches.

And then they heard it—**a low, guttural growl**, followed by **a whisper that wasn't quite human.**

"**She marked you.**"

A figure appeared at the edge of the clearing—a **twisted, humanoid shape**, covered in rags and branches. Its face was **long and featureless**, except for a mouth twisted into a jagged grin.

The Ruben had come to claim its mark.

Haruto grabbed Aiko's hand, and they ran, the Ruben's footsteps thudding behind them like the **heartbeat of the forest itself.** The trees closed in, branches snagging at their clothes, trying to **pull them into the earth.**

Aiko's breathing became ragged, her legs burning with every step. **"It's getting closer,"** she gasped, her voice barely audible over the whispers swirling around them.

Haruto pulled her along, refusing to slow down. **"We're almost out!"** he lied, though he knew they were hopelessly lost.

Just when they thought they were free, **the Tattered Girl appeared again**, standing in the path ahead of them—her hair covering her face, her hands hanging limp at her sides. **Her head tilted, as if she were waiting.**

Aiko knew what the legends said—**once the Tattered Girl marks you, there's no escape.** But the legends also mentioned **one way out:**

"If you give her a gift, she'll take it in your place."

"We have to give her something!" Aiko cried, her voice breaking with fear.

Haruto fumbled with his camera, panic clouding his thoughts. **"What do we have?"** he asked, glancing frantically at Aiko.

And then it hit her—**the bracelet** her grandmother had given her, said to protect the wearer from harm. It was the only thing she had that mattered.

With shaking hands, **Aiko pulled off the bracelet** and threw it at the Tattered Girl's feet.

The girl tilted her head again, her long hair swaying. Then, slowly, **she knelt and picked up the bracelet**, slipping it over her wrist.

The moment the bracelet touched the Tattered Girl's wrist, **the forest fell silent.** The fog lifted, and the Ruben—**with one** final, menacing growl—melted into the shadows, vanishing into the darkness.

Aiko and Haruto stood there, panting, their hearts still racing. **The Tattered Girl was gone.**

Without a word, they turned and **ran toward the village**, not stopping until they reached the safety of the inn.

That night, Aiko lay awake, staring at the ceiling. **She could still feel the cold touch on her hand**, like the mark had never really left.

And just before she drifted off to sleep, **she heard a whisper**—soft and distant, but unmistakable:

"I'll see you again... next October."

The Forgotten City

In the heart of Cincinnati, two cities existed side by side, separated by a towering **dividing wall**. On one side, life thrived with modern skyscrapers, bustling streets, and people living their busy lives. On the other side lay **the Old City**—a shadow of its former self, abandoned, crumbling, and consumed by wild overgrowth.

The Old City was a place of tragedy. Fifty years ago, a **freight train carrying letters, parcels, and gifts** derailed as it thundered through the heart of the district. The train crashed into apartments and homes, setting off fires and collapsing entire buildings. The devastation was immense, and many families perished that night, buried under rubble and steel. Some were asleep in their beds. Others, enjoying dinner with loved ones, were caught in an instant of horror.

The bodies were pulled from the wreckage, but the spirits, it seemed, had never left. **Ghostly sightings** began soon after—figures glimpsed at windows, disembodied voices whispering from abandoned homes, and strange knocks that echoed through the dead streets at night. The survivors fled, and no one returned to rebuild.

To contain the restless spirits, city officials erected a **great wall** around the ruined district. **Priests blessed it**, praying it would keep the spirits confined. Over time, the Old City was forgotten—**a ghost town left to the past.**

But curiosity has a way of creeping into the minds of the young, and **four teenagers—Danny, Ava, Tyler, and Maya—were about to discover** that the dead are not so easily confined.

"I still say it's all bullshit," Danny muttered, kicking a loose stone as he walked. They stood at the foot of the **dividing wall**, the iron gate rusted shut, draped in ivy and decay. The night sky was cloudy, the October air crisp and biting.

"You don't really believe all that stuff about ghosts, do you?" Ava asked, though her voice wavered.

Tyler chuckled nervously. "I don't know, man. If the city built a whole wall and brought in priests... there had to be a reason."

Maya, the quiet one, stared through the gate, her flashlight beam slicing into the dark streets beyond. "It's just a ghost story," she whispered, more to herself than anyone else.

Danny grinned, pulling a crowbar from his backpack. "Only one way to find out."

With a loud **creak**, the iron gate groaned open. A gust of cold air rushed through, carrying with it the faint scent of smoke and... something older. **The smell of forgotten things.**

"After you, fearless leader," Ava whispered, nudging Danny forward.

And just like that, they slipped into **the Forgotten City**.

The streets of the Old City were eerie and silent. Vines crawled up the walls of buildings, broken windows gaped like empty eye sockets, and old streetlamps stood crooked, their bulbs long dead. The train tracks, warped and twisted, ran like scars through the city.

"It's like time stopped," Tyler whispered. "Like everything just... froze."

Maya shivered, her flashlight catching glimpses of **old signs and doorways** half-swallowed by ivy. The shadows pressed closer, as if the darkness were alive, waiting to pounce.

They reached the **crash site**, where the remnants of the train still lay—a tangled mess of metal, wood, and debris. Letters and parcels lay scattered across the ground, untouched for decades. Some of the letters looked strangely intact, as if they had only just been delivered.

"That's weird," Ava said, kneeling to pick up an envelope. "It's got my name on it."

Danny grabbed another. His heart stopped. "This one's... mine."

They scrambled, tearing through the envelopes. **Each letter bore their names, written in neat, old-fashioned handwriting.** Even more unsettling, **the letters described their deaths**—each one more horrifying than the last.

Tyler read aloud, his hands trembling. "You'll run, but you won't make it. The wall... the wall won't let you leave."

Danny scoffed, though his bravado was cracking. "It's just some sick prank. Someone got here before us."

But deep down, they all knew—**no one had been in the Old City for fifty years.**

Then they heard it—the distant **whistle of a train**, long and mournful, cutting through the silence.

"Do you hear that?" Maya whispered, her breath fogging in the cold air.

The whistle grew louder, accompanied by the rhythmic **clatter of wheels on tracks.** They turned toward the twisted rails, and that's when they saw it—**the Ghost Train.**

It emerged slowly from the darkness, a spectral locomotive glowing faintly under the pale moonlight. **Inside the shattered cars**, ghostly figures sat motionless—pale, translucent faces staring out through broken windows.

One by one, the spirits **turned their hollow eyes toward the teenagers**. Their lips moved in silent whispers, and though no sound came from their mouths, the words echoed in the air:

"Join us. Stay with us."

A figure in the front car—a **woman clutching a child**—lifted her hand and pointed directly at Maya. The others followed suit, their fingers rising in unison, pointing at each of the teens.

"They see us," Ava whispered, her voice trembling.

"Run," Danny breathed. **"RUN!"**

They bolted down the dark streets, their footsteps pounding against the cracked pavement. The Ghost Train followed, its whistle blaring louder, the clattering wheels growing faster.

Maya risked a glance behind them—and wished she hadn't. **The spirits were no longer on the train.** They **ran alongside it,** their twisted limbs jerking unnaturally as they pursued the teenagers through the crumbling city.

Ava screamed as **ghostly hands** reached out from the shadows, grasping at her clothes. Danny swung his crowbar wildly, but the spirits melted away only to reappear just a few steps ahead.

"There! The gate!" Tyler shouted, pointing toward the dividing wall. The rusted gate stood open, just a few yards away, but the air seemed to **thicken,** slowing their every step.

The whispers grew louder, swirling in the air:

"You belong to us now. Stay with us... forever."

They reached the gate just as **the first ghostly hand** wrapped around Danny's arm, pulling him back. He swung the crowbar with all his strength, breaking free. Ava and Tyler pushed through the gate, gasping for breath.

Maya was right behind them—**but the gate slammed shut.**

"Maya!" Ava screamed, tugging at the bars. "Open it! Hurry!"

But Maya stood frozen on the other side, her eyes wide with terror. **The spirits surrounded her,** whispering softly, gently, like old friends welcoming her home.

"You came," they murmured. "And now you stay."

Danny grabbed the gate, yanking it with all his might. "No! Maya, hold on!"

But it was too late. **The spirits closed in**, their pale hands resting on Maya's shoulders, pulling her into the darkness. The last thing they saw was her terrified face, her hand reaching for them—and then, she was gone.

The gate swung open again, but **Maya was nowhere to be found**. The Old City stood silent once more, the Ghost Train vanished, the whispers fading into the wind.

Ava collapsed, sobbing. Tyler stared at the empty street, his face pale with shock. Danny stood in silence, gripping the crowbar until his knuckles turned white.

They made it back to the other side of the wall, but none of them would ever speak of what happened. No one would believe them, anyway.

A few days later, **a letter appeared in Danny's mailbox**. It was addressed to him in neat, old-fashioned handwriting.

Inside was a single line:

"We are waiting."

The End.

Bonus: Kamrucho Daily

The **Kamrucho prefecture in Japan** was not a place for the faint-hearted. Known for its **crime syndicates, underground fight clubs, and murky back alleys,** the streets buzzed with **secrets, danger, and betrayal.** Amidst this chaos was **Detective Ryo Kurogane,** a man as feared as the criminals he hunted. With his expertise in **Mixed Martial Arts (M.M.A.)** and a reputation for **solving impossible cases,** Ryo was the kind of detective you didn't mess with—because **he didn't back down. Ever.**

But this time, things were different. What started as a **routine investigation** was about to become a fight for survival.

The case came to Ryo through **a newspaper called the Kamrucho Daily.** It was an ordinary tabloid—known more for gossip than investigative journalism—but this particular story caught his eye:

"Teenage Girl Goes Missing—Last Seen Near Kamrucho Market."

Something about the report didn't sit right with Ryo. The **girl's name was Hana Fujimoto,** and she wasn't just anyone—**she was the mayor's niece.** If she had gone missing, why was this being treated as **tabloid fodder** instead of a **full-blown police investigation?**

Ryo felt his instincts kick in. He knew something bigger was going on, and **he wasn't going to let it slide.**

His investigation led him deep into **Kamrucho's underbelly.** Hana had been spotted near **an underground fight club**, a place Ryo knew all too well. He had fought there himself years ago—back when the ring was his sanctuary from the chaos of the streets.

Ryo entered the club that night, blending seamlessly into the crowd of fighters and gamblers. **The smell of sweat and blood hung heavy in the air**, and the audience roared as fists flew inside the cage.

Ryo wasn't there to fight, but when **a familiar face challenged him**—one of his old rivals from the ring—he didn't hesitate. **A few precise strikes**, a brutal grapple, and Ryo had the man pinned in under a minute.

"Where's the girl?" Ryo growled, tightening his grip.

The man coughed, trying to catch his breath. **"She's not what you think,"** he whispered. **"You're going to need more than fists to survive this."**

Ryo soon discovered that **Hana's disappearance** wasn't random. She had stumbled upon **something dangerous—a web of corruption involving powerful figures, local crime lords, and police officials.**

The Kamrucho Daily had tried to report the truth, but every time they got close, someone intervened. Now, with **Hana missing**, Ryo was walking into **a trap set by the very people he once trusted.**

As he pieced the puzzle together, Ryo found himself in **a race against time.** If he didn't find Hana soon, she would **disappear for good.**

The trail led Ryo to an **abandoned warehouse on the outskirts of the city.** Inside, he found Hana—**tied to a chair, her eyes wide with fear.**

But before he could free her, the door slammed shut, and **six armed men stepped out of the shadows.** They were hired muscle—trained fighters, each one ready to kill.

Ryo cracked his knuckles. **"Let's dance,"** he muttered under his breath.

What followed was **a brutal, high-octane brawl**, a symphony of fists, kicks, and grapples. Ryo fought with precision, using every technique he knew—**from jiu-jitsu locks to Muay Thai strikes.**

One by one, the men fell, until **only Ryo was left standing**—battered, bruised, but victorious.

Ryo untied Hana and carried her out of the warehouse, the **first rays of morning light breaking over Kamrucho.** She looked up at him, her face pale but relieved.

"You're safe now," Ryo whispered, brushing a strand of hair from her face. **"Let's get you home."**

Later that day, **the Kamrucho Daily** ran the story that no one else dared to print. **The real truth**—about Hana's kidnapping, the corruption, and the fight Ryo had to endure to save her. The headline read:

"Detective Saves the Day—Kamrucho's Hero Returns."

Ryo smiled as he folded the paper. For once, **the city had a happy ending.**

Bonus: 1ˢᵗ Grade

It was **October in Manchester**, and the autumn chill swept through the streets, ushering in the season of **falling leaves and creeping shadows**. For most, it was a time for pumpkin patches and Halloween decorations, but for **Ella Parker**, it was a season she would never forget—a season that began with **her son's first-grade class** and ended with a nightmare she could never wake from.

Ella had been excited for her son, **Jamie**, to start first grade. He was always curious, full of life, and eager to learn. On the first day of October, she walked him to **Creston Primary School**, where his teacher, **Mrs. Whitlock**, greeted them with a warm smile.

Everything seemed normal—**too normal**, as Ella would later think. The classroom smelled of fresh crayons and paper, and cheerful drawings of pumpkins and skeletons lined the walls. But there was something odd about the way Mrs. Whitlock watched her students—**like she was counting something** in her mind.

As the day ended, Jamie ran into his mother's arms, laughing and chatting about **new friends and fun games**. But **something had changed**—just a flicker in his eyes, too faint for Ella to understand at the time.

A week later, **the nightmares started.**

Jamie would wake up in the middle of the night, crying about **a boy who sat at the back of the classroom**—a boy who didn't speak, didn't play, and never left his seat.

"He watches me," Jamie whispered one night, his small voice trembling. **"He's always there. Even when the lights go off, he's there."**

Ella tried to comfort him, but as the nights wore on, the nightmares grew worse. Jamie began **drawing strange pictures,** showing a **shadowy figure with hollow eyes,** always watching from the corner of the page. And every morning, Ella noticed that **Jamie's behavior grew more distant** each day. He was no longer the cheerful boy she knew—his face looked pale, and dark circles formed under his eyes. Every morning before school, he would cry, begging Ella not to make him go.

"He's waiting for me," Jamie whispered one morning, clutching Ella's arm. **"The boy at the back. He doesn't blink, Mum. He never blinks."**

Ella spoke to **Mrs. Whitlock,** hoping to get some answers. But the teacher's warm demeanor seemed off. **Her smile didn't quite reach her eyes,** and her reassurances felt scripted. **"There's no boy like that in my class,"** she said, tilting her head as if amused. **"I think Jamie has an overactive imagination."**

The drawings Jamie made became more disturbing. **Figures grew taller and thinner,** their limbs twisted and elongated. In each picture, **Jamie drew himself smaller,** surrounded by these creatures.

One day, Ella found a new drawing hidden under his bed. **It wasn't a child's scribble anymore**—the lines were precise, as if drawn by an adult. It depicted **a classroom filled with faceless children**, and at the back sat **a boy with hollow eyes**, staring directly at Jamie.

Beneath the picture, in messy handwriting, were the words: **"You can't leave."**

Ella's concern turned to fear. That night, she called the school to ask about the boy at the back of the classroom. **The receptionist hesitated before answering.**

"Mrs. Whitlock's class? It's odd you mention that," she said. **"There is an empty desk at the back of the room—has been for years. But no one ever sits there."**

Ella's blood ran cold. She knew something was terribly wrong, but the receptionist couldn't—or wouldn't—tell her more.

Determined to get answers, **Ella decided to visit the school after hours.** She parked outside the building, waiting until the staff had left, and then slipped inside. **The hallways were eerily quiet**, the only sound the faint hum of fluorescent lights overhead.

She found her way to Mrs. Whitlock's classroom and opened the door slowly, her heart pounding in her chest. The classroom was dark, the desks neatly arranged—**except for one.**

At the back of the room, **the boy's desk sat askew**, as if someone had recently used it. The air around it felt **cold and heavy**, and as Ella stepped closer, she saw something that made her stomach churn: **Jamie's name was etched into the desk, carved deep into the wood.**

As Ella turned to leave, **a whisper drifted through the room—** soft, distant, like a child's voice carried on the wind. **"He can't leave. Not until you take his place."**

Ella froze. **The classroom door swung shut with a heavy thud**, and the temperature in the room plummeted. **The lights flickered**, and when they came back on, **she wasn't alone.**

Sitting at the boy's desk was **the figure Jamie had described**—a pale, hollow-eyed boy dressed in an old, tattered uniform. He smiled, but there was **no warmth in it**, only emptiness.

"I was here first," the boy whispered. **"I'm not supposed to leave... but he can stay for me."**

Ella's heart pounded as the truth hit her: **The boy was a spirit, trapped in the classroom for years, waiting for someone to take his place.** Jamie had somehow caught his attention—and now, the boy wanted **Jamie to stay forever.**

Ella felt the room closing in around her, the air thick with unseen pressure. **She had only one chance**—if she didn't act, she would lose Jamie to the shadow of this forgotten child.

"Take me," Ella whispered, tears streaming down her face. **"Leave my son alone."**

The boy tilted his head, considering her offer. Then, slowly, he smiled.

When Ella woke up, she found herself sitting in the front seat of her car, parked outside the school. **The sun was rising, casting a golden glow over the city.** For a moment, she wondered if it had all been a dream—but then she looked at **the back seat.**

Jamie was there, fast asleep, his face peaceful for the first time in weeks.

She reached out to touch him, relief flooding through her. But as she did, **she noticed something odd**: Jamie's small hand clutched a piece of paper.

Unfolding it, Ella's breath caught in her throat. **It was another drawing—a classroom, empty, except for one desk at the back.**

Sitting at that desk was **a woman,** her face drawn in precise, familiar lines.

It was **Ella herself.**

At **Creston Primary**, Mrs. Whitlock's classroom was quiet as the students filed in that morning. Everything was back to normal—or so it seemed.

As the children sat down, **Mrs. Whitlock glanced at the back of the room,** a small smile curling at the corners of her lips.

The empty desk was finally occupied.

DID YOU KNOW?

- The Baby

  Did you know? In many cultures, spirits are believed to mimic the sound of babies to lure people into danger.

- The Cursed Tree

  In Romania, there are legends of trees that trap souls—anyone who harms them falls under a generational curse.

- The Film That Wasn't There

  Early horror films were often destroyed or "lost"... some say for reasons that had nothing to do with storage.

- The Gallows

  Execution sites in Europe were often left untouched for centuries—locals claimed the soil was cursed.

- The Return of Daisy

  In folklore, pets returning after death is a known omen—especially if their eyes don't reflect light.

- The Final Ritual

  Did you know? In ancient Mesopotamia, failed rituals were believed to trap spirits between worlds—forever.

- The Man in the Mirror

  In Victorian times, mirrors were covered after someone died—to prevent their soul from being reflected and trapped.

- The Fog That Followed

  "Sentient fog" is a recurring theme in urban legends worldwide—from San Francisco to the Scottish Highlands.

- The Profile That Posted Itself

  There have been real reports of dead people's social media profiles coming back to life due to hacking—or something else.

- The Broadcast

  During the Cold War, strange unexplained signals were picked up across Europe—some believe they weren't human in origin.